I0517488

Demon

Between the Realms

Book 1

N.C. Madigan

Between the Realms: Demon
Copyright © 2022 by N.C. Madigan.

All rights reserved. Printed in the United States of America. No part of this book may be used or reproduced in any manner whatsoever without written permission except in the case of brief quotations embodied in critical articles or reviews.

This book is a work of fiction. Names, characters, businesses, organizations, places, events and incidents either are the product of the author's imagination or are used fictitiously. Any resemblance to actual persons, living or dead, events, or locales is entirely coincidental.

For information contact:
contact@ncmadigan.com
www.ncmadigan.com

Cover design by Eve Evans
Book Formatting by Derek Murphy @Creativindie

ISBN: 979-8-9850617-5-8

First Edition: October 2022

10 9 8 7 6 5 4 3 2 1

DEMON

N.C. MADIGAN

Chapter One

BLACK COFFEE

Lucas Harrison sat in an armchair, his feet propped on the scuffed-up coffee table. The coffee shop was busier than normal for an early afternoon - perhaps the lunch crowd was running late. He watched the line of business-casual patrons place their orders, pay, and wait at the end of the counter for their low-fat iced mochas, or whatever it was people ordered these days. Cappufrappamochalattenowhipwhateverthefuckwithsoymilk.

A gentle wafting presence appeared beside his shoulder.

"What is it?" he asked, keeping his voice low. He didn't need the other patrons thinking he was talking to himself. He was already receiving dirty looks from the corporate pions, probably because of his long hair and scruffy appearance in a high-end coffee shop.

"Why are you still here?" an ethereal voice asked him. Lucas lolled his head to the side. Rosie Black, one of his newer Clingers, a lost spirit between worlds, hovered beside him, looking around the coffee shop.

"Why not?"

"I'm bored."

Lucas rolled his eyes. "I'm not your entertainer," he replied. Rosie huffed.

"You said that we could go stalk my ex-boyfriend," she replied, prodding him in the arm. He could feel the pressure from her finger - she was as close to a full corporeal spirit as a Clinger could get. Lucas was rather impressed.

"Did I say that?" Lucas asked, taking a long drink of his lukewarm black coffee. Rosie huffed again.

"I don't wanna be stuck with you for all eternity," Rosie whined. "I want to cross over."

"And you really think that finding out if your ex is sleeping with your former best friend is really the best way to do that?" Lucas asked. Rosie didn't answer right away. When Lucas looked back at her, he found that she had fixed him with a dark glare. He smiled. "Alright, alright. We'll go stalk him."

Lucas pushed himself up from the chair and downed the last of his coffee. He grabbed his bag, slung it over his shoulders, and left the coffee shop, depositing his cup in the trash on his way out.

Out in the sunlight, Rosie's form nearly disappeared, and Lucas's only clue that she was still beside him was the feeling of a presence. That, and she wouldn't stop prodding him in the arm.

"We're going, we're going," Lucas protested, waving his arm in her general direction. He felt a pinch on his arm.

"I told you not to grope me," Rosie said.

"And I told you that Clingers can't be groped." Lucas marched down the sidewalk, leaving Rosie to catch up to him.

She'd already told him where her ex-boyfriend lived in the city, so he used his phone's GPS to locate it and work out a walking path to the apartment building. Beside him, Rosie continued to chatter to herself. When she'd first become attached to him, he'd tried to keep up with her rapid speech. He eventually realized she didn't want answers and that it was simply her way of dealing with her problems. And so he ignored her.

About halfway to the ex-boyfriend's place, Rosie tugged on Lucas's sweatshirt.

"What now?"

"Margaret is back," Rosie said. Lucas winced. He turned down the next alley and waited. Sure enough, a wailing filled his ears, and a young woman appeared in front of him, her 1850s wedding dress torn and covered with dark blood spots. She paced up and down the alley, her ethereal wailing echoing off the buildings.

"Margaret, please stop," Lucas begged, but she ignored him. Margaret liked to pretend she was a residual spirit, destined to perform the same ritual over and over, forever. She had Lucas convinced that it was true for a long time until he caught her admiring some clothes in a shop window.

"My wedding is supposed to begin soon! Where is my dear future husband?" she wailed, her hands pressed to her breast. Rosie shifted angrily beside Lucas, stirring up a bit of garbage on the ground. Lucas held out a hand to Rosie, indicating that she should calm down. With a sigh, Lucas took a deep breath, closed his eyes, and took a step forward.

He felt the soft brushing of the living realm disappear as he entered the cold spirit realm. When he opened his eyes, all color was gone - replaced with shades of gray - and all sounds were muted. On this side, he could see Margaret almost as she'd been on the day she died. Spirits appeared more substantial on their own side of existence.

Margaret stopped wailing and stared at Lucas, her dark eyes annoyed.

"You care so little for me now," she complained. "She's taking up all your time with her silly revenge ideas." Lucas sighed inwardly, and Rosie barked a laugh.

"You don't even want to cross over, and your dear murdering

husband has been dead for like, hundreds of years," Rosie countered. Lucas held up his hands, palms facing each of the two women.

"Calm down, ladies. Margaret, remember that I'm not your fiance. I'm your caretaker," he said. Margaret crossed her arms over her chest and turned her chin away.

"My last caretaker was much kinder," she protested. "He made me so happy." Lucas raised an eyebrow.

"He killed himself," Lucas reminded her. Rosie burst into laughter. "You drove him to suicide?"

Margaret threw herself forward, intent on attacking Rosie. Lucas dug a bundle of strings from his pocket and held one out, pulling it taut between his fingers. Margaret froze when the string began to glow.

"Margaret, I'm pretty sure the entire realm knows that you're not a residual spirit, so drop the act permanently. Go calm down. You can come back when you're ready to behave," Lucas commanded. The forsaken bride huffed and turned away. Her form shimmered until it was confined to the string in Lucas's hands, which glowed pink, then returned to white.

"She's so nuts," Rosie said.

"You're on thin ice too, Miss," Lucas said, and Rosie shut her mouth. Shoving the strings back into his pocket, Lucas stepped back into the living realm. The sounds of the city overwhelmed his ears, and the light and colors blinded him for a moment. He waited until his senses readjusted, then stepped out of the alley and onto the sidewalk.

"Let's go," he commanded to Rosie, who returned to his side.

The ex-boyfriend's apartment building was situated in a nicer part of town, with a doorman guarding the front door. Lucas slowed his walk. "How are we supposed to get in there?" Lucas asked.

"Tell him you're a repairman or something for apartment 1309," Rosie suggested. It was as good an idea as any. Lucas approached the doorman.

"I'm here to fix a computer in apartment 1309," Lucas said to the doorman, who stared him down for a moment, obviously wondering at the validity of his statement.

"Alright," the doorman said. He pushed open the door and allowed Lucas to pass though. He walked across the pristine lobby to the bank of elevators and punched the UP button. Several seconds passed, during which Lucas rocked unsteadily on his feet. He wasn't keen on confronting Rosie's ex-boyfriend; after all, he had no stake in their relationship. But if he wanted to lessen his workload, he needed to help those Clingers who could be and wanted to be helped.

At least, that's what the grim reaper had said.

A soft ding indicated an elevator had arrived, and a set of silver doors slid apart. Lucas boarded the elevator and pushed the button for the 13th floor.

"I was always surprised they even had a thirteenth floor in this building," Rosie said.

"That's such a dumb superstition," Lucas said. The elevator rose steadily up thirteen stories and halted. The doors opened again, and Rosie left first, guiding Lucas down the hall to apartment 1309. At the door, Rosie waited. She could have just passed through the door, but she had yet to grow accustomed to her own death. And if her confrontation with her ex-boyfriend went well, perhaps she wouldn't have to worry about it. Perhaps she could cross over.

"You can go in," he said. Rosie wrung her hands in front of her.

"I'm nervous," she admitted, casting her eyes at the floor.

Lucas reached out to her shoulder, an automatic gesture of comforting, which had little effect, but the intent was understood. Rosie took an unnecessary deep breath and floated through the door.

Chapter Two

REVENGE

Lucas waited outside the door. He felt her energy moving around inside the apartment and heard a scream; he didn't know whether it had come from Rosie or some other woman. Lucas knew that Rosie could cause a commotion if she really wanted to, considering how substantial her spirit form was. If she had been angrier in life, she might have ended up as a poltergeist.

He could hear pounding and a general cacophony of noise. Rosie must be having a fit. Lucas sighed, leaned against the wall beside the door, and crossed his arms over his chest. He didn't know how long this was going to take.

To Lucas' surprise, the apartment building door flew open and a young man and a young woman stumbled out. Both were naked, clutching blankets and sheets around their bodies. Lucas pressed himself back against the wall, his hands splayed on either side of his hips. Without saying anything to him, barely even noticing that he was there, the man and woman ran screaming down the hallway towards the elevator. Curious, Lucas peeked through the open door.

The inside of the apartment was completely trashed. Chairs and tables were overturned, plates and dishes lay on the floor, some cracked, and lamps lay on their sides, the bulbs busted out. Impressive work.

Lucas raised his eyebrows when he heard cackling laughter beside him. Rosie had appeared at his side.

"That'll show 'em," she said. Lucas glanced at her semi-transparent form.

"So, was it what you expected?" he asked. Rosie nodded.

"They are sleeping together. But I think I gave them enough of a scare," she said. Lucas smiled.

"Think you're ready to let go?" he asked.

"Yes, but not here. Let's go to the park."

* * *

Lucas led the way to the nearest park, a small patch of greenery surrounded by cement and buildings. Lucas found a bench along a stone path and sat down, resting his bag beside him to discourage anyone else from sitting beside him. Not that anyone would, but he didn't think Rosie would take too kindly to being sat on.

Lucas watched as children played on the play structure while mothers either paid attention to the children or their cell phones. A few people in athletic gear jogged past him along the dirt path. A group of elderly men and women sat together, talking and playing chess.

"Thanks again, Lucas," Rosie said, her voice soft as the breeze blew through the trees.

"Of course. It's my job," he replied.

"It means more to me than just crossing over," Rosie said. "Even though I'm still disappointed, at least I know the truth."

"And that's enough for you?" Lucas asked.

"Yeah, I suppose. I mean, I'm going to miss out on a lot of life," Rosie said, heaving a sigh. "But if I had stayed home that night instead of leaving to find out where he was and who he was with, I wouldn't be having this conversation with you." Silence fell. Lucas wasn't sure what to say to comfort the young woman.

"Do you know what happens after we cross over?" Rosie asked.

"Sorry, I don't," Lucas replied. "Even the grim reaper wouldn't tell me. So I didn't get much of a choice when he asked me to be a caretaker to you clingers."

'That's a shitty deal," Rosie commented, and Lucas shrugged his shoulders.

"I try not to think about it too much."

Silence fell once more, and Lucas contented himself with watching the activity in the park. As he sat on the bench, he could feel Rosie's energy fade away, a little at a time. After each passing moment, she became less substantial. Lucas thought he heard Rosie say something, but her voice was carried away by the wind. A few more minutes passed, and her energy was gone. Lucas smiled to himself and pulled his wad of strings from his pocket. He pulled out the one that Rosie had been attached to. It was dark. She crossed over to the other side.

Chapter Three

OPERA GHOST

Lucas sat in the back of the auditorium, his arms crossed over his chest. He wasn't even sure why he was there-- there was some free symphonic concert that he had seen online. And once Margaret had heard about it, she demanded they go, less she resume her awful screeching. He could feel her presence at his shoulder, waiting anxiously for the concert to begin.

On stage, the chairs were set up in semi-circular rows. Large white panels were set up behind the chairs to enhance the sound and volume of the musicians. Black music stands stood interspersed among the chairs, and one large music stand, along with a podium, was set up in front of the rows. Lucas couldn't even remember the last time he'd listened to symphonic music. His tastes tended to run in the metal variety.

Another presence made itself known at Lucas's other shoulder. He sighed to himself. It was Rocko, one of his angier clingers. Today, however, he didn't feel angry, just annoyed.

"Lucas."

"Hi, Rocko," Lucas said, turning his head to look in the direction of the spirit. Rocko's form could be seen only by the distortion of the space beyond him.

"There's something here," Rocko said. "Something malicious."

"Are you sure it isn't you?" Margaret asked. Before Rocko could retort, Lucas pulled out his strings, threatening the two to behave.

"Don't even start," he said. "Go on, Rocko."

"It's an angry spirit," Rocko said. "Maybe a poltergeist." Lucas frowned.

"That's no good," he said, rising up from his chair. The auditorium was filling with people, and surely the musicians were in the building somewhere, preparing for their show. A restless spirit could cause a very public display if it wanted to. "Margaret, you stay here and keep a lookout for any trouble. Come get me if you see anything."

Margaret sighed. "As you say."

"Let's go, Rocko," Lucas said and followed the other spirit down the row of seats. When Rocko passed by some of the spectators, they shuddered involuntarily from his chilly energy. "Where do you think it is?"

"Somewhere backstage," Rocko said. They moved down the steps toward the stage. A few ushers lingered near the house doors. Lucas halted for a moment and looked around. He wondered if there was a way to access the back of the stage from outside the auditorium.

"This way," he said and walked through the house doors and back into the lobby.

The lobby was full of people chatting and looking at pictures of the musicians. The lights in the lobby dimmed briefly, which spurred the crowd towards the doors of the auditorium. The show would be starting soon. Lucas hurried through the crowd, searching for a door that would lead backstage.

Finally, he found a set of doors near the bathrooms. The doors were unguarded by ushers. Lucas casually bumped into the doors, and they opened. He looked around, knowing how suspicious he looked, but pushed his way through the doors, closing them silently to avoid attracting attention.

"This would be easier if you were a spirit," Rocko commented, floating through the wall. Lucas ignored him.

He found himself in a long, empty hallway. He walked down the hall, passing by large garage doors on either side of him. The hallway broke off in another direction, and it was then he heard the sounds of footsteps and whispered chatter. Lucas shrank back, peeking around the corner. A line of musicians dressed in black and carrying their instruments walked down the other hallway and disappeared through an open door. Lucas watched them, waiting until they had all gone on stage.

Rocko alerted him by wafting gently near Lucas' elbow.

"There's someone coming from behind you," he said. Lucas glanced over his shoulder. A man in a dress shirt and slacks appeared, striding down the hallway, his phone pressed to his ear. Lucas ducked around the corner and threw open the nearest door. He found himself in a tiny vestibule. Lucas tested the next door, which was also unlocked. He slipped through, gently closing the door behind him.

He was backstage. It was dark, save for the lights on the front of the stage seeping through gaps in the curtains. Lucas turned and tiptoed across the back of the stage, where he could see the musicians entering from the hallway. They were still filing into their seats. Against the very back wall of the stage, Lucas found a small area where he could hide. Crouching down, he waited.

"Do you see anything, Rocko?" Lucas whispered.

"I can feel it, but I can't tell where it's coming from," Rocko answered. "Whatever this is - it's a very powerful spirit."

"Great," Lucas mumbled. He drew out his wad of strings from his pocket and shifted through them. Most of the strings glowed faintly, meaning the clingers contained within were peaceful or hanging out in the spirit realm. The two dark strings were Margaret's and Rocko's. "I have a full group," Lucas said. "I couldn't capture this spirit if I wanted to."

"Maybe I can wrestle it back to the other side to at least keep these people from getting hurt," Rocko suggested. Lucas raised his eyebrows.

"Since when do you care about anyone else?" he asked. He could sense Rocko's embarrassment.

"These people aren't the source of my anger," Rocko said, sounding a little sheepish. Lucas smiled but dropped the issue, not wanting to lose the help of this powerful spirit. Settling himself in the little cubby hole, he and Rocko waited.

* * *

The orchestra music filled the backstage area, and Lucas closed his eyes, enjoying the songs they played. They weren't the normal drab songs that his grandmother used to play on the radio-- these were powerful, upbeat songs that made Lucas ready to jump into action at any moment.

If only the spirit would reveal itself.

Lucas shouldn't have wished for anything. As soon as the thought passed through his mind, he heard a loud clatter from nearby. Lucas jumped to his feet, with Rocko at the ready. "Over there," Rocko said, pushing Lucas toward the sound. Lucas crept along the wall, avoiding stacks of stage lights, cables, and other junk piled along the wall. Lying on the floor was a metal light stand-- Lucas thought maybe that's what had made the noise.

"He's here," Rocko said. Lucas looked around, but he couldn't see anything. Rocko disappeared from Lucas's side.

"Hey! Where are you going?" Lucas called in a loud whisper. But Rocko was already gone, and above his head, Lucas could see the curtains rustling. "Come back here, Rocko!" he called, but Rocko ignored him. He was already engaged with the other spirit.

Rocko wasn't strong enough. The rustling of the curtains stopped, and Lucas felt the strings in his pocket warm. He pulled out the wad and saw that Rocko's glowed. He had returned to the spirit world. "Shit." Looking up, he saw something, the outline of a figure, up above the stage.

Then he heard the snap. The heavy bar that held the curtain fell, swinging down in an arc, still holding onto the remaining lines that held the bar up above the stage. Then another snap and the bar swung lower. Lucas leaped to the side, his legs tangling in the next curtain. He wrestled with the heavy fabric, trying to free himself. Another snap and the bar crashed onto the stage, sending a heavy reverberating note into the air. The orchestra on stage ceased playing, and people in the audience began to shout and scream. Lucas freed himself from the curtain and climbed up to his feet. Hovering above the falling curtain was a spirit - in the form of a tall man. Lucas could feel emanating evil.

"Lucas! Are you hurt?" a soft voice asked him. Margaret had returned to his side. "What happened?"

"Go away, Margaret. This spirit is too strong for you," Lucas said. Margaret touched his shoulder.

"But-"

"Go!" Lucas commanded, his voice crossing to the spirit world, forcing Margaret to obey. She disappeared, and the string in his pocket warmed.

"Ah-- a caretaker," the spirit said. The sound of its voice sent shivers up and down Lucas's body.

"What are you doing here?" Lucas asked, drawing himself up. He'd have to keep bluffing his way through - there was nothing he could do against this spirit except hope that Rocko had enough energy to return.

"That's none of your business," the spirit answered. Lucas was about to reply when the spirit threw himself at Lucas, passing through his body and leaving him cold and weak. The spirit stole some of his energy. Lucas dropped to one knee, his breath now passing rapidly through his lungs.

"What's going on back here?" a voice called. Lucas looked up. He saw the well-dressed man from before. He'd skidded through the door onto the stage, his phone in hand and at the ready. Lucas shook his head.

"Get out of here!"

"This is my stage!" the man shouted.

"It's dangerous!"

Lucas heard three snaps, all in a row, and another curtain crashed down towards the stage. Lucas pushed himself out of the way while the other man dodged the falling bar.

"What the hell?"

Lucas forced himself back to his feet, though his body shook with the effort. He drew out his strings and looked at them. Rocko's was still dim; he wasn't strong enough to cross back over to the living world just yet. And none of his other spirits would even come close. There was nothing he could do.

Snap snap snap

Another curtain fell. The screaming around him increased, and he could see the musicians running toward the back of the stage, their instruments clutched to their chests. The curtain hit the white panels, knocking them down, and crushing chairs and music stands. Lucas looked around; the man with the phone had disappeared. A wailing tone erupted over the loudspeakers - a fire alarm. Good enough. At least it would get everyone out of the building.

Lucas was ready to give up and leave when he felt the presence of another spirit-- a strong one, but not malicious. He looked around and saw the energy fly towards the very top of the ceiling over the stage. Where had that spirit come from?

"Get out of here!" a voice shouted. A woman appeared from the curtains. She wore a summer dress, her blonde hair pulled back into a bun on the back of her head. She was in her late twenties, maybe a few years younger than Lucas. A large bag was slung across her chest, resting against her hip. In her hands, she held two wads of strings.

Another caretaker?

"To protect and release!" Lucas called over to her. Slowly, her head turned back towards him, her eyes wide.

"...The souls left behind," she finished. A worry line formed between her eyebrows. She opened her mouth but shook her head. "Let me take care of this," she shouted. Her head snapped back to look up at the ceiling. She pulled a string taut between her fingers, and another spirit formed in front of her. It flew up toward the ceiling.

Lucas could feel the clashing of the spirits above him, their energies pulsating back and forth. The woman felt for another string, and a third spirit materialized in front of her. This one, too, flew up toward the ceiling. Lucas crept closer to the woman, who was focusing intently on the battle waging above their heads. He watched as she drew a length of wire from her bag and held it in her hands.

"Bring him down!" she shouted, and with a terrible rushing noise, four figures descended from the ceiling - three holding onto the struggling spirit. Lucas heard the woman chant something in Latin. The wire in her hands glowed, and gradually, the evil energy of the spirit disappeared. When it was gone, the woman twisted the wire, forming a knot in the middle. It continued to glow, but the brightness dimmed slightly. She stowed the wire in her bag and looked up at her spirits. "You can go back now," she said. "Thank you." Without a word, the spirits disappeared, their strings glowing in her hands.

Lucas hadn't realized he was now staring at her with his mouth hanging open. The woman glanced at him and sighed.

"Let's get out of here before the police show up. I don't think you want to have to explain anything, either," she said. Lucas nodded, forcing his mouth closed. The woman motioned for him to follow her, and they walked across the stage, emerging at the front. The auditorium was completely emptied. The woman led him back through the doors to the lobby, and exited out a side door that Lucas hadn't noticed. Outside, Lucas jogged to catch up to her. She strode towards a white sedan, which was haphazardly and illegally parked near the door.

"Get in," she commanded, and Lucas obeyed, tossing his bag into the backseat and climbing into the passenger seat. She slipped into the driver's seat, adjusted the skirt of her dress, and started the car.

"You're a caretaker?" she asked him, after she'd navigated out of the parking lot and onto the main road.

"Yeah-- and you? I've never seen the kind of thing you did there," Lucas said, the words falling out of his mouth faster than he could manage. For the first time, the woman smiled slightly.

"I'm a special class of caretaker," she explained. "I get the worst kinds of spirits."

"But you had spirits who helped you," Lucas said.

"Yes, I have a few. They used to be angry spirits, but I counseled them to help me," the young woman explained. Lucas raised a brow.

"You got them to change their energies?" he asked, and she nodded her head. "That's amazing!"

The young woman shrugged. "It's not that hard."

"Well, I'm impressed. My name is Lucas Harrison." She glanced at him.

"Kira Sterling."

Chapter Four

GRIM

Kira drove her car into an abandoned parking lot. Beyond was an old warehouse of some kind. Most of the windows had been busted out by rocks or weather. Kira parked the car and stepped out. "Where are we?" Lucas asked.

"There's a grim reaper who hangs out around here. I need to drop off this spirit," Kira said. The two caretakers climbed out of the car, and Lucas followed Kira toward the warehouse.

"Have you been a caretaker for a long time?" Lucas asked, but Kira just shrugged her shoulders lightly. She pulled a chain off the handles of a door and threw it open. A musty, damp smell wafted from the warehouse. Lucas covered his nose and followed Kira as she strode inside.

"You can cross, right?" she asked, not looking at him.

"Yeah, of course."

"Come on, then."

Lucas followed her lead; closing his eyes and taking a deep breath, he took a step forward and felt the familiar brushing of the barrier between the living and the dead. Opening his eyes, he stood beside Kira in the spirit world. Now that he was on this side, he felt the presence of his spirits gathering around him. Margaret appeared beside him.

"What happened to the spirit?" she whispered to him. Lucas gestured at Kira.

"She caught him in a piece of wire," he answered. Kira glanced at Margaret, then at Lucas.

"One of your charges?" Kira asked with a smirk.

"I intend to haunt him until he dies," Margaret said, sticking her nose in the air and turning away. Kira chuckled, then her expression turned serious.

"Dukaru!" Kira shouted. "I've got another one!"

"Dukaru?" Lucas asked.

"He's a grim reaper," Kira said. From her bag, she dug out the piece of wire with a knot in the middle. It glowed and vibrated with energy. The air around them snapped and grew colder than cold. Goosebumps formed all along Lucas' exposed skin. Dust and leaves on the floor began to swirl, and in the middle stood a robed figure, a dark hood pulled up and over its face. The robe swirled around its body, dissolving into a mist near where the figure's feet should be. Darkness enveloped the spirit realm.

It was a grim reaper.

Lucas hadn't actually seen one since the day he was given a choice to die or become a caretaker. He shuddered. Margaret's presence retreated away from the reaper.

"You found it?" the grim reaper asked, gliding towards Kira. His voice sounded like falling rocks. Kira nodded and held out her hand. The grim reaper reached out and picked up the wire with a skeletal hand. Lucas couldn't remember his grim reaper being quite this creepy or cliche. In fact, Lucas's grim reaper had looked like an ordinary man. "How much trouble did it cause?" the grim reaper asked.

"Interrupted a concert, brought down several curtains. I left before anyone saw me," Kira explained. The grim reaper examined the wire and stowed it away in its robe.

"Your payment will be put in the usual account." Kira nodded, and in a swirl of dirt and black mist, the grim reaper disappeared.

"Hold on. Payment?" Lucas asked. Kira turned to face him.

"There are some perks to what I do," she said. "The downside is being at the beck and call of the grim reapers at all hours." Kira sighed and stretched her arms over her head. "I could use a drink. Want to come along?"

Lucas stared at her, then nodded.

"Sure."

Chapter Five

MARTINI

Kira drove the two of them to a small pub that Lucas had never heard of before. Upon entering, it was clear that Kira was a regular when the bartender hailed her by name. She walked ahead and hopped up onto a stool, pulling at her skirt to keep the fabric around her knees. Lucas followed and climbed onto the stool beside her.

"The usual?" the young woman behind the counter asked. Kira nodded. "And you?" the bartender asked, looking at Lucas.

"Whatever IPA you've got on tap," Lucas said. The bartender nodded and moved away. Lucas turned to Kira. "When are you going to answer my questions?" he asked.

Kira sighed and rested her chin in her hand.

"I don't really know you," she said. Lucas rolled his eyes.

"How many friends do you have?" he asked. "How many people understand the life of a caretaker?" Kira frowned.

"No one," she answered.

"Don't you get lonely?" She didn't answer right away. The bartender set down a martini with two olives in front of Kira and a pint glass of beer in front of Lucas.

"I guess," she mumbled.

"We can be friends," Lucas said. "I've never met another caretaker before." He took a long sip of his beer. The silence between them was uncomfortable, so Lucas spoke. "Five years ago, I was hit by a truck. I fell into a coma for several months. I knew I was hovering between life and death. Then one night, I woke up from the coma - or at least my soul did. A grim reaper was in my hospital room, looking at me. He asked if I wanted to live. Of course, I told him I did. He said if I agreed to become a spirit caretaker, he'd send my soul back to my body, and I'd go on living until such time as I should die... again.

"I didn't have time for a lot of questions, but I agreed, and my soul was sent back to my body. I woke up from the coma and spent several more months in the hospital. When I left, I returned home to find a bundle of strings on my bed.

"People don't really know what to say to you when you essentially come back from the dead. And once I learned more about being a caretaker, my friendships and relationships fell away. It wasn't them - I stopped calling people and making an effort. My spirits became my companions."

When he finished, Kira bit her lower lip and looked away.

"I guess I have a similar story..." she said. Lucas could tell she was reluctant to tell him any of it.

"You don't have to tell me now," Lucas said. "But at least let us be friends. I'm sure we could help each other out." Lucas watched Kira have an inner war with herself until she finally smiled.

"Alright. Friends."

Chapter Six

PLANS

Lucas lived in an apartment on the top floor of a three-story building. The second floor was another apartment, and the main floor was a sex-toy shop.

The apartment was a seven-hundred-square-foot studio. The only enclosed area was the bathroom. The rest of the apartment was open and contained his bed, a dresser, a few mismatched old couches and chairs, a rickety coffee table, and a bookshelf that was over-stuffed with books. Since becoming a caretaker, Lucas had taken to reading books about the spirit world and theories on death, both pseudo-scientific and religious. He read these books to laugh at how wrong they were.

Upon entering his apartment, his head was still a little buzzed from his drinks with Kira. Lucas dumped his bag on the floor and sprawled out on his bed. He was exhausted from the excitement of the day and was ready to sleep. Unfortunately, his spirits were in a talkative mood.

Rocko, Margaret, and one of his older clingers, Thomas, appeared in his room. Thomas was a burly black man who was murdered for the simple crime of being black. Lucas didn't think Thomas would ever cross over.

His spirits stared at him expectantly.

"What?" Lucas asked, lifting his head from the bed.

"That young lady is strange," Margaret said, her hands planted on her hips.

"How was she able to stop that spirit?" Rocko asked. Thomas just stood by, interested.

Lucas waved his hands. "I don't know. She didn't discuss her techniques with me. All I know is that she can use wire to contain the very unruly spirits. I think she is maybe assigned to catch them," he said.

"She had spirits fighting for her," Rocko said. "Why don't you use us like that?" Lucas pushed himself into a sitting position.

"We don't fight evil spirits. Besides, it would have to be your decision," Lucas said. Rocko and Thomas exchanged glances.

"I want to help!" Rocko said, thrusting a fist into an open palm. The blankets on Lucas' bed fluttered. "You should try and get the same deal as that girl."

Margaret startled Lucas by agreeing. "It would certainly liven things up." Lucas raised an eyebrow.

"Thomas?" he said, turning to look at the third spirit, who had been silent thus far.

"My unfinished business will never be finished. I wouldn't mind having something to do while I'm stuck in this place for all eternity," Thomas said, his voice sounding distant.

"I'll try to talk to her, then, about whatever it is she is doing," Lucas said. "No bailing on me, though." The spirits smiled and disappeared. Lucas groaned and curled his body up onto the bed. What was he getting himself into?

Chapter Seven

DATING SITES

Kira had made it very clear that she was a very private person. Therefore, Lucas didn't try contacting her right away, lest he scare her away. A week passed before he finally heard from her. During that time, Lucas had helped two of his more docile clingers pass on and gained a new one, a young boy who insisted on being called Clark Kent. Lucas was fairly certain Clark Kent was a residual spirit, as the boy didn't seem to realize he was dead.

Kids always made Lucas feel terrible.

When Kira finally contacted him, Lucas was lazing around his apartment, reading a recently purchased book about hauntings in famous locations around the world. It was an amusing book, and Lucas thought if he ever had the money, he'd like to visit these supposedly haunted places and find out for himself.

Lucas's phone buzzed, indicating a text message. He reached blindly for the device and pulled up the text. It read, "want to get a drink?" He grunted in surprise. He replied in the affirmative, and she asked for his address.

Setting aside his book, Lucas dragged himself to his feet and wandered into the bathroom. He relieved himself, then glanced in the mirror. He didn't look great; he wet his hands and tried to smooth out his hair a little. He didn't bother trimming his beard. It would take too long.

Back in his room, he changed into clean clothes and slung his bag over his shoulder. He didn't know how long it would take Kira to reach his place. He paced his apartment and mused how his spirits weren't popping out to bother him right before she arrived. They usually picked the most inopportune times to say hello. In fact, they'd been quiet all day. Even Margaret.

The buzzer to his apartment went off. Lucas strode to the panel on the wall and pressed the button to release the door. He heard it open and slam closed, and a moment later, Kira's head appeared at the top of the stairs. She smiled tentatively.

"You live here? Above a sex toy store?" she asked, looking around the mostly barren apartment. Lucas shrugged.

"As you might imagine, I don't spend much time here," he replied. Kira wandered his apartment, pausing at his bookshelf. Lucas watched her, amused.

"You don't believe the shit in these books, do you?" she asked, looking over her shoulder at him. Lucas shook his head.

"Of course not. They make me laugh." Satisfied by this, Kira turned her head back to the bookshelf and looked over the books for a moment, mouthing the titles silently. She turned back to Lucas.

"Let's go," she said and walked towards the steps. Lucas stared after her for a moment, wondering what had prompted such a strange, rather nosy assessment of his apartment. Perhaps she was still sizing him up? Lucas shrugged to himself and followed Kira down the steps.

In the car, the two sat in awkward silence until Lucas finally decided to break it.

"Did you... have a tough week?" he asked, trying to sound nonchalant.

"You could say that," she answered.

"You know that I'm dying to hear more about your work. Uh, no pun intended," Lucas said, and he saw her grimace before turning her head to look at him.

"I'm still deciding whether or not I trust you with that information," she replied.

"Even though I'm also a caretaker?"

"Yes. It's not just you, Lucas. I have problems trusting most people," she said. "Getting drinks is one thing," she continued before Lucas could protest. "But sharing secrets and intimate details is something completely different."

"Does it have anything to do with how you became a caretaker?" he asked. She pursed her lips together for a moment before replying.

"Something like that." Lucas let the subject drop. Kira surprised him by asking a question of her own. "Do you work?"

"No. I tried for a little while after my recovery, but it got too weird with the clingers always hanging around."

"What do you live off?" she asked.

"The settlement I got from the truck driver who hit me. Living frugally, I can make ends meet every month with a small stipend," Lucas explained. "At least for a little while longer."

"I see. Do you uh - have a girlfriend or anything?" she asked, and Lucas could see she was blushing at her own question. He gave her a darkly skeptical look.

"What do you think?" he asked. Her blush darkened. She began to apologize when Lucas cut her off. "I'm just kidding. But no, of course not. Maybe we could create a dating website for caretakers. Call it the Spirit Connection or something," Lucas said. Kira snorted.

"Yeah, I'm sure that would go over well. You'd end up with a whole lot of weirdos," she said, giving him a sly glance. Instead of retorting, Lucas just laughed, and to his surprise, Kira laughed along with him.

Chapter Eight

PAST

Kira took them to the same bar they had visited the week prior. "Why this place?" Lucas asked while they climbed out of her car.

"It's discreet," she said. "And you know, once the bartender knows your favorite drink, it's hard to stop frequenting the place, don't you think?"

"I've never been to a place that many times," Lucas replied. Kira shrugged and led the way into the bar.

The bartender was different this time, but he apparently knew Kira as well. She chose a barstool, and the bartender was already pulling out a jar of olives and a martini glass. After he set the drink down in front of Kira, he turned to Lucas. "What are you drinking?"

"Whatever IPA you've got on tap," Lucas replied. When the bartender turned away, Lucas leaned his chin on his hand. He waited for Kira to take a drink of her martini. "So, how was work then?" he asked.

"Just the usual. Angry spirits everywhere. I had a poltergeist this week, too. That was loads of fun," she said. The bartender returned with a glass of beer and set it on a napkin in front of Lucas.

"Do you ever get children?" Lucas asked.

"No," she answered, shaking her head. She tilted her head slightly. "Do you?"

"Yeah, sometimes. I have one right now. It's kind of heartbreaking, you know, to explain to a six-year-old that they're no longer alive."

Kira frowned, a sad expression crossing over her face. "You're a braver person than I. There's no way I could do that."

"It's not easy, and they're some of the hardest to convince to pass on," he said. "Once you convince them that they're dead, they want to have all this communication with their family, which isn't possible, you know." Kira nodded. "And some don't want to leave their toys behind."

"How do you get around that one?"

"I tell them there are a lot more toys on the other side," Lucas said.

"Are there?"

"No clue."

They chuckled for a moment before once again dissolving into silence. Kira reached the bottom of her martini glass, and a moment later, the bartender was back with a second. After another sip, she angled her body towards Lucas.

"Alright - here it goes…" she began. Lucas raised an eyebrow but waited patiently. "I have technically died four times."

"What?!"

"Yeah, and those four times, I have been saved by a grim reaper - that one you met, in fact."

"But I thought-"

"That after the second time, it's over? That's how it's supposed to go," Kira said. "But for some reason, Dukaru allowed me to live on the condition that I do his dirty work of catching the unruly and dangerous spirits."

"His dirty work…"

"He's supposed to be doing it all himself, but he has a few hired caretakers, like me, to help him out. This city is just teeming with angry and vengeful spirits. He also has some old woman working for him - that's who sends over the payments for catching the spirits."

"How does a grim reaper get real money?" Lucas asked.

"I have no idea," Kira said. "He won't tell me, and I don't know the real identity of this person who sends me the money. I have learned not to ask too many questions."

"When was the first time you died?" Lucas asked. Kira's expression darkened, but she answered him.

"I was five years old. I was... my parents were fighting. My dad pulled his handgun on my mom and tried to shoot her, but he missed and hit me instead." Lucas's mouth dropped open, and his hand clenched around his glass so hard he thought it might break. "While I was in the hospital, I died, and that's when I met Dukaru. He didn't make me a full caretaker then - I was much too young. But he taught me several basics in that short amount of time and sent me on my way back to the living."

"What happened with your parents?" Lucas asked quietly.

"My dad did kill my mom, and he was sent away to prison. I went to live with my grandmother." Kira downed the rest of her drink and hailed the bartender for another. "I was ten when I was supposed to die again. I got really sick, and when I was teetering between life and death, Dukaru returned. He said he could save me again if I would be willing to help him. For some reason, I agreed. I guess I wasn't ready to die yet. That's when I received my first bundle of strings and my first few spirits."

Lucas's stomach churned. He pushed away his beer glass, leaving a few swallows at the bottom. He thought he might vomit if he tried to finish.

"The next time, I was sixteen. I just got my driver's license. I was hit head-on by a semi-truck that had hopped the median between the highway. I was still pinned inside my car when Dukaru appeared, shaking his head and saying that I was accident-prone. This was when he made me the deal - he would continue to keep me alive if I helped him trap the worst kinds of spirits. He said I'd get paid for my work, and he would train me. I don't know why I agreed, but I did. Dukaru sent my spirit back to my body, and I made it through the accident alive.

"The most recent time was two years ago when I was twenty-four. You know how we caretakers are not the most socially adept people-" Lucas nodded. "Well, I fell into a bad crowd and began dating this guy. He was a drinker and drug user, and he had a terrible temper. One night, something happened that pissed him off, and he took out his anger on me. Dukaru actually came to my rescue that time. He killed my boyfriend and trapped his spirit, thereby saving my life. And now, I'm bound to Dukaru for as long as my body can hold up in the living world." Kira paused a moment. "That's my story. That's why I am the way I am."

Lucas sat stunned for several minutes, replaying parts of her story in his mind. Lucas hadn't known that grim reapers could affect the living by actually killing them. That was new. It made sense why she was so reluctant to make any friends. He wondered what sort of infatuation this grim reaper had with her to keep her alive so many times. It was suspicious.

"Dukaru trained me to deal with the angry spirits and how to catch them in the wires. He taught me the knots to tie forcibly to bind them into confinement. And…"

"And what?"

"I can force spirits to the other side."

"Wouldn't that make you a grim reaper yourself?" Lucas asked, stunned. Kira smiled.

"Nearly. I believe when I do die, that's where I'll end up."

Lucas shook his head, hardly believing what she was saying. He didn't know that much about the whole process - he didn't have a connection with a grim reaper like she did. But he wondered what made her stand out against all the others that were near death. Perhaps there was some other power or energy that Kira possessed that made her a perfect de-facto grim reaper.

"I can tell this is freaking you out," she said.

"A little. Just realizing there's so much I don't know," Lucas said. Kira smiled shyly and turned back to her drink. "I have a million questions and can't think of which one I want to ask first."

"It's doubtful I'll have the answers anyway," Kira said. She finished off her third martini. Lucas saw the flush creeping up on her chest, her eyes were glazed, and the pinkness in her cheeks stood out against her pale skin. There was no way she was going to drive herself home. At least not anytime soon.

Chapter Nine

EVIL

As Lucas was musing on what to do, Kira swore loudly and reached into her purse. She removed her phone and looked down at the screen. "There's a spirit nearby. I need to get it," she said, hopping off her barstool, and swaying on her feet.

"Hold on. You're drunk, Kira," Lucas said. "You can't do this right now." Kira snorted.

"I have done this drunk hundreds of times." Kira reached into her purse and pulled out a wad of bills, which she tossed on the counter. Lucas searched out the bartender, but he smiled and waved them out the door. Lucas grabbed Kira's arm and led her outside into the fading sunlight. She pulled a pair of sunglasses from her purse and pushed them up her nose.

"I'm driving," Lucas said, plucking her keys from her hand. She protested, but he overpowered her, thrusting her into the passenger seat of her car. He climbed into the driver's seat and turned over the engine. Kira looked down at her phone.

"The abandoned building at 5th and Highland road," she said.

Lucas nodded and maneuvered the car onto the street and in the direction of the spirit. As he drove, he noticed that the part of the city they were in got worse and worse, with more abandoned buildings, transient-looking people, and suspicious characters. When he reached the crossroads, he saw the large building, which must have been an office building at one time. High up on one of the floors, the lights flashed erratically. Lucas pulled the car down an alley and turned off the engine.

"Are you sure you can do this?" he asked her. Kira nodded and climbed unsteadily out of the car, stumbling

"I can't really die, can I," she reminded him. Lucas frowned, but he grabbed his bundle of strings from his bag and slipped them into his pocket. He followed Kira from the alley and to the boarded-up front door of the building. "Can you pull these boards down?" she asked.

Lucas gripped the edges of the plywood and yanked. It came away easily from the nails, and Lucas leaned board on the side of the building. The air released from the building was dank and musty. Lucas pulled a handkerchief out of his pocket and wrapped it around his mouth and nose, a lesson he'd learned the hard way. To his surprise, Kira did the same thing. She crossed the threshold and motioned for him to follow her.

The lobby of the building looked frozen in time. Seventies colors, decor, and furniture were evidence of the last time the building had been used for its original purpose. Loose papers had blown around the floor, mingling with dust and dead animal carcasses. Kira led the way across the lobby towards the stairwell. She removed a flashlight from her purse and illuminated the area.

"Fly ahead, please, and figure out which floor it's on," she said, a string in her hand from her bundle. Lucas felt the presence of a spirit appear, then grow fainter as it ascended up through the building, looking for the angry spirit. For good measure, Lucas removed his bundle and found Rocko's string. He didn't think that the spirit would be as strong as Kira's, but at least Lucas would have some sort of protection. Lucas called on Rocko, who appeared instantly at his side.

"What do you need me to do, boss?" Rocko asked, flexing his ghostly muscles.

"Just stay near me," Lucas whispered. "Watch out for whatever spirit is lurking here."

"Sure thing."

Kira climbed up the stairs, and Lucas hurried to follow. Their footsteps on the concrete stairs echoed up the stairwell, announcing their presence to any living being that might be hiding in the building. Up and up, they climbed until Kira's spirit returned.

"Twentieth floor," a deep voice said. Lucas could feel the spirit's eyes on him.

"Thanks. Keep ahead in case it decides to join us here. What is it?" Kira asked.

"Standard poltergeist, I think," the voice replied. Kira nodded, her fingers dancing through her bag until they reappeared, clutching a wire. She manipulated the wire between her fingers. Lucas wondered if it was standard practice or if she was nervous.

With many more floors to climb, they continued on their way, both Kira and Lucas dragging their feet after about ten floors. Finally, they reached the twentieth floor, and Lucas thought his legs were going to fall off. They pushed through the door into the hallway, and both collapsed on the ground, sending up a large cloud of dust and grime from the old carpet.

Lucas felt Rocko go on high alert. "I can hear him," Rocko said.

"Indeed," Kira's spirit answered. Lucas listened but heard nothing out of the ordinary. "Follow me." Lucas dragged himself to his feet, and he offered a hand to Kira, who looked soberer though she smelled of gin. He hoisted her to her feet, and they walked down the hall, following Kira's spirit.

Before long, Lucas began to sense the incredible energy of the poltergeist. At that moment, Lucas was thankful for his rather mundane job as a caretaker. His angriest spirits were Margaret and Rocko. He couldn't even imagine hunting down anything angrier than those two.

The lights on the floor flashed on and off, and doors rattled in their frames. Kira's spirit led them to a door and stopped moving. "He's in there for the moment."

Kira clutched the wire in her hand and threw open the door.

Lucas and Kira both took an involuntary step back as a blast of air hit them hard in the chest. Lucas felt himself pass through Rocko as he stumbled backward.

"What is that?" Lucas cried out.

"He's pissed!" Kira replied. The angry, whirling squeal of the poltergeist filled their ears. Inside the room, the lights blinked on and off erratically while a cyclone of energy ripped up papers, furniture, dust, animal skeletons, and other bits from the floor and tossed them around the room. A chair busted through one of the windows with a crash, and Lucas could see, in his mind's eye, the chair falling to the ground and smashing into tiny pieces on the sidewalk.

"Can you subdue him?!" Kira shouted to her spirit.

"I will try," the voice answered. Rocko hovered beside Lucas once again.

"Should I help?" he asked.

"I don't know. I get the feeling her spirits aren't used to outside help," Lucas said. Rocko understood and remained by Lucas's side.

Kira stared intently into the room, watching the flurry of activity. The cyclone died down a bit, though furniture continued to smash against the walls and windows. There was an apparent clash between the two spirits, and Lucas felt Kira's spirit energy disappear.

"What happened?" she asked out loud. Rocko shouted, and he, too, disappeared.

"Hey! Come back here!" Lucas shouted to his spirit.

Rocko reappeared for a second, but only to shout the words, "That's a demon!"

Chapter Ten

DEMON

Lucas and Kira glanced at each other, their movements slow. Fear radiated from Kira.

"Is he telling the truth?" she asked in a whisper.

"I don't know."

Inside the room, all the activity stopped, and the silence weighed heavily. Lucas was about to ask if the spirit was gone, but a harsh voice, speaking words in a language Lucas didn't know, cut through the brief silence. They both stared into the room, and a figure materialized before their eyes. It was a grotesque shape, humanoid, with horns and broken wings, a long, horse-like face, and cloven hooves. Sharp teeth jutted out from its mouth, which dripped with something. Its burning red eyes stared across the room at them, and before they could react, it flung itself forward, intent on attacking. Lucas and Kira threw their arms up uselessly to protect themselves, screaming.

But nothing happened. Lucas lowered his arms and looked around. Kira was still beside him, cowering beneath her arms. Lucas touched her elbow, and she looked up. "We're in the spirit realm," he said in a soft voice. Kira looked around.

"How did we get here?" she asked. Rocko and Kira's spirit appeared before them to answer her question, looking solid.

"I hope you'll forgive me, mistress," Kira's spirit said. "We felt it was necessary to pull you to this side to protect you from the demon." Lucas stared at the spirit. He was a large man with dark skin and heavy features. His voice was ringed with a slight accent.

"That's alright, Reis," Kira said, her shoulders relaxing slightly. Reis bowed his head. Lucas sighed heavily and dropped down to the ground. Rocko knelt beside him. Lucas could feel his other spirits nearby, remaining out of sight.

"You should try to get out of here, boss," Rocko said. "I know you can't travel far in the spirit world, but you should at least try to get out of this building." Lucas removed his wad of strings from his pocket and slipped them through his fingers, thinking.

"Can you trap a demon?" Lucas asked Kira. She shrugged.

"I have never been sent to catch one," she said.

"It would require additional supplies," Reis said. "Demons are different than spirits. They have more substance and therefore require a stronger prison."

"I don't think you should try again," Rocko said, glancing between the other three. "You could end up dead."

Lucas was at a loss. He didn't want to be killed, but he also didn't want to let that demon run free. Kira sighed.

"There's nothing we can do right now," she said. "Reis, can you try to contact Dukaru and let him know that it's not a poltergeist here?" Reis nodded and drifted away, eventually disappearing entirely.

"Let me guide you out of this building," Rocko insisted. Lucas nodded and rose to his feet. Kira was swaying on hers, so he looped his arm around her waist to steady her. With Rocko leading the way,

Lucas and Kira made their way slowly through the spirit world, down the steps toward the first floor of the building.

Walking in the spirit world, for humans, was similar to walking through deep, heavy mud. It required much more effort, and it was a definite possibility that a human could over-exert him or herself and die in the spirit world. Lucas didn't want to know what would happen to his own spirit should that happen.

Halfway down the steps, Lucas and Kira had to pause for a break. Rocko waited nearby, nervously twisting his fingers. Lucas rarely saw Rocko so nervous. That was usually reserved for Margaret. Rocko glanced up the steps as if expecting the demon to appear at any moment.

"Is he still here?" Lucas asked.

"Yes," Rocko breathed. "He's angry. But I think he might be stuck in this building. Once you're outside, you should be safer."

"Can you keep going, Kira?" Lucas asked. Kira nodded her head, but she was slipping away from consciousness. Lucas hoisted her up, and with a steady arm around her, they continued their slow descent down the steps.

The passage of time in the spirit realm differed greatly from the living realm. Lucas had no idea how long it took them to reach the first floor. The hands on his watch stopped. When they rounded a corner, the next door had a large black "1" painted on it, and Lucas sighed in relief. He picked up his pace, pulling Kira along with him, through the door and across the lobby. Rocko jumped ahead, waiting for them to pass through. Once they were outside, Lucas could feel the last of his energy slipping away.

"You have to go now. Cross back over," Rocko insisted. Lucas nodded and shook Kira. Her heavy eyes opened.

"Come on, Kira. We have to cross," he urged. She nodded, and together, they closed their eyes and took a step. The barrier allowed them through, and in the next moment, they were standing in the living realm. Colors and sounds returned in full force. The hands of Lucas' watch jumped forward to read two o'clock in the morning. Thankfully, Kira's car was still parked in the street.

"Get home safely, okay, boss?" Rocko said, his form barely visible. Lucas nodded.

"Thanks, Rocko. Stick with Reis if you can. He seems to have a lot of information we could use."

"Sure thing."

Rocko disappeared. Lucas hauled Kira to the car, pulled open the door, and tried to put her in the passenger seat as gently as possible. Once he had her strapped in, he walked around to the driver's side door. He slipped inside and started up the engine. He hoped he could find his way back to his apartment.

It took about an hour to navigate his way through the streets. When he arrived at his apartment, he parked Kira's car in the alley beside the building and pulled her from the passenger side. She hadn't moved since they left the building, and Lucas was beginning to worry. With the last remaining strength, he hoisted the girl up in his arms and carried her up the steps to his apartment. Inside, he laid her on his bed and pulled the blankets up around her. For a moment, he considered perching himself on the other side of the bed, but he thought she'd kick his ass in the morning. Instead, Lucas grabbed an extra blanket and pillow and retreated to the couch. There, he fell asleep as soon as his eyes closed.

Chapter Eleven

HANGOVER

The thick sound of retching woke Lucas. He dragged open his eyes and rolled off the couch onto his feet. Still half asleep, he stumbled towards the bathroom, whose door was still open. He found Kira leaning over the toilet, her hair a jumbled mess. She coughed once, then heaved into the toilet again. Lucas perched himself on the edge of the bathtub and swept her hair back. When Kira realized he was there, she groaned and tried to move away.

"Just get it all out," Lucas ordered her. She made a noise of protest, but it was interrupted by another wave of retching. She coughed again and spit something from her mouth.

"What happened?" she asked, leaning her face to the side, propped up on her arm. Her eyes were bleary and clouded.

"What do you remember?"

"The demon. He came after us, and then I must have blacked out." Lucas told her what happened after that, about their slow progress through the spirit world, and how he drove her back to the apartment. He reminded her that she'd sent Reis to find Dukaru.

Kira groaned.

"That's why I feel terrible," she said. Lucas raised an eyebrow. "The spirit world doesn't agree with me."

"That's strange."

She shrugged. "No one has ever had a reason for me. I try to stay on this side. Even Dukaru doesn't know why."

Lucas stared at her, thinking. He gave that endeavor up quickly - he was too exhausted to try and figure anything out. Turning, he twisted the knob for the shower. "Do you have enough energy to shower?" he asked her. Kira shrugged, but she flushed the toilet and rose to her feet, using the wall for support. "I'll make some coffee while you do that. If you need anything, just yell." Reaching up, he pulled down a towel from the metal rack bolted to the wall and set it on the edge of the sink. Kira watched him silently until he stepped out of the bathroom and closed the door.

The demon plagued his mind. They couldn't just let that go. It would have to be captured, killed, or whatever it was that removed demons from the land of the living.

Lucas wandered into the kitchen to make coffee. He retrieved two ceramic mugs from a cupboard and fished out the half-and-half from the fridge. While the little machine popped and bubbled, Lucas leaned against the counter and ate a banana. How to destroy a demon?

His eyes landed on his bookshelf. A seed of an idea formed in his mind. Dropping the banana peel in the trash, he walked to the shelf and scanned the spines of his books. He knew he had a demon book somewhere. He found it on the bottom shelf, stuck in next to an old copy of the Bible that he hadn't been able to get rid of. His grandmother had given it to him back when he believed in that sort of thing. Her handwriting covered the first page, and now that she was gone, Lucas couldn't bear the thought of throwing the book away.

Shifting his thoughts back to the problem at hand, he removed the book about demons and let it fall open in his hands. Colorful pictures of demons graced every few pages while black text shone out on the glossy white paper. He flipped through, scanning the pages and # Chapter titles. Most of the information was historical-- accounts of demons in religions and cultures from around the world. Some more modern anecdotes. A discussion about the symbolism often portrayed in paintings of demons. Lucas' idea was deflating quickly until he flipped to the back cover. On the dust jacket, he saw the picture and short biography of the author. The picture showed an African-American man with short-cut hair and dark eyes. It looked like he was wearing the costume of a Catholic priest, but Lucas wasn't sure. Lucas read the bio beneath the picture

> *Isaiah Aquino has a Master's degree in theology and has studied the concept of demons present in many religions and cultures. He currently lives in Chicago, Illinois, where he banishes demons and spirits from homes, buildings, and people.*

Lucas's idea didn't feel so crazy anymore. Below the biography was a website address. He carried the book to his desk and set the book down, dropping a paperweight on it to keep the pages open. From the bathroom, he heard the water shut off. While he waited for Kira to emerge from the bathroom, he booted up his laptop.

Kira opened the door and stepped out of the bathroom, surrounded by steam. Lucas smiled.

"Feeling better?" he asked.

"Slightly," she said. Her wet hair hung loosely around her face, dripping onto her shoulders and sundress. Lucas motioned for her to follow him, and he poured a cup of coffee for her. She dumped in half-and-half and sugar and took a long drink from the cup. Lucas waited, the coffee pot in hand until she lowered the cup and held it out for a refill. Lucas obliged, then filled his own cup. Kira hoisted herself up on one of the barstools.

"So I had a thought," Lucas said, leaning on the counter opposite from her. Kira raised her eyebrows.

"About?"

"The demon."

"Right."

"I know you don't believe in human ideas about the dead--" he began, receiving the eyeroll that he expected. "But I thought we might need a little help dealing with this demon."

"What kind of help?"

"Someone who can banish spirits and demons," Lucas said. Kira sighed and pressed a hand to her face.

"Come on, Lucas. That stuff is all shit," she protested.

"I know, but I think it's worth a try." He watched her struggle with the idea, clearly hating it but offering no other alternatives.

"Do you know someone?"

"I know of someone," Lucas said. He walked back to his desk and picked up the book. He set it down in front of her on the counter. "I bet we could contact this guy and see if he could fly out here." Kira flipped through the book, then skipped ahead to the dust jacket. She rolled her eyes again.

"There's no way this guy is legit," she said. Lucas waited, smiling gently. She thumbed through the book once more, taking long sips of coffee. He noticed that her face still looked slightly pale. He supposed they ought to get food soon. Kira closed the book and looked up at him. "Dukaru doesn't care about demons. Once he learns this particular entity isn't a spirit, he's going to cross it off his list, so to speak. Technically, we don't have to do anything about it. It's not our job."

"I can't just let a demon remain on our side," Lucas said, his voice firm. Kira groaned and looked away. "I also can't do this alone. You have skills I don't have." Kira remained silent for several minutes while she apparently thought it over. She ran her hands down her face and shifted her gaze back to his.

"Alright. I'll help. But you will owe me a lot of drinks afterward," she said. Lucas grinned.

"Deal." He reached out to shake her hand, and she obliged. Lucas had assumed that she would make some kind of demand, but he honestly thought she'd demand that he leave her alone. Drinks he could handle.

Chapter Twelve

TITANIUM

After breakfast at a nearby diner, they returned to Lucas' apartment. Kira flung herself back on his bed, declaring herself too tired to drive home. Lucas grabbed the book from the counter and sat down in front of his laptop. He typed in the URL from the dust jacket and perused Isaiah Aquino's website. It was loaded with photos and stories about various demons and spirits he'd banished, along with snippets from his books. There were also several dates listed when he would be speaking at a convention or conference. None of the locations were nearby.

It took some time, but Lucas eventually found an email address for Isaiah. Of course, he had to search the source code for the email address-- a rookie mistake on Isaiah's part. Lucas brought up his own email and typed an email to the proclaimed demon banisher, explaining the situation without giving away too many details of Kira and Lucas' positions as caretakers. Lucas was going to have Kira read it over before he sent it, but she was fast asleep on the bed. Hoping for the best, Lucas sent along the email to Isaiah.

* * *

Lucas was reading through Isaiah Aquino's book again when Kira finally woke up. Some of the paleness had left her face, and her eyes looked brighter. Lucas was about to speak when he felt a spirit presence that wasn't one of his own. Kira sat up in the bed and looked to the side, where the spirit was hovering.

"Reis? Did you find Dukaru?" she asked.

"Yes, mistress. He wasn't happy to hear that the poltergeist was actually a demon," Reis replied. Kira rolled her eyes.

"Did he say anything useful?"

"Only 'titanium,'" Reis said. Kira looked like she wanted to protest, but instead she tilted her head to the side.

"I guess that makes sense. Thanks, Reis," she said. In the next moment, Reis' presence was gone. Kira shifted her gaze to Lucas. "I need titanium wire."

"For the demon?" She nodded. "That seems too easy." Kira snorted.

"You've never trapped the type of spirits I go after. They're much more difficult to trap. If I'm supposed to catch this demon in wire, then I imagine it will be difficult to subdue it to a point where he's weak enough to be trapped." Kira paused, her eyes lifting to the ceiling. "In fact, I'm not sure if a spirit can weaken a demon. They're not exactly on the same plane of existence."

Lucas rose from his chair and began to pace across the floor, a frown on his face. "That does pose a problem," he said. "If this Aqua guy is the real deal-"

"Probably not." Lucas shot Kira a look.

"If he's the real deal, he might have some advice on how to take this demon down." Kira was frowning deeply, but she pushed herself off the bed and stood before Lucas, halting his pacing.

"Look, I know you want to help, but this could be extremely dangerous," she said.

"I thought we already discussed this," he replied.

"I know, but I just don't think you fully understand," Kira said, her voice almost pleading. "If you die, there's no guarantee that your grim reaper will bring you back again like Dukaru has done for me. Spirits can affect us minimally, depending on their power, but they must cross the barrier between their world and ours, weakening any residual power they might have. Demons are different. They exist in a completely different world, one that is much closer to ours, leaving them with more power over the living."

"You've never encountered a demon before?" Lucas asked.

"No."

"How do you know all this?"

"Dukaru has told me some things over the years about what I might expect while doing this shit job," Kira replied. "Up until now, it's never been something I couldn't handle." Lucas frowned and began to turn away, but Kira grabbed his arm and squeezed it tightly. "We had a deal, I know. But I need an amendment to that."

"Which is…?" Lucas asked, his eyes dropping to stare at her pale hand, which was still squeezing his arm.

"If I tell you to get the hell out, you must go," Kira said. Lucas looked up to her face. "I'm serious." The blush on her face was unmistakable. Lucas covered her hand with his own.

"Alright, fine. I promise," he said. Kira sighed in relief and released the hold on his arm. Lucas watched her turn around and pick up her purse from the ground.

"I'm going to look for titanium wire after I go home and change," Kira said. "I'll uh… call you later or something."

"Sure."

Kira nodded to him and hurried to the steps. Lucas watched her disappear and waited until he heard the slam of the door below. He shook his head, feeling confused and concerned. As if reading his thoughts, Margaret appeared at his side.

"She likes you."

"Go away, Margaret," Lucas said, heading towards the bathroom, shedding his clothes as he walked. He knew Margaret would hate it. She scoffed.

"You are a vile man," Margaret said, and her presence disappeared. Lucas chuckled to himself and stepped into the narrow shower stall, content to remain there as long as the hot water held out.

Chapter Thirteen

AQUINO

The following day, Lucas was wandering the city streets, his phone in his hand. He'd glance down at it every few minutes and alter his course. He had received a message that he was to find a wandering spirit hanging onto an old pawn shop, but the exact pawn shop was unknown. Using his phone, Lucas had mapped out a route to all the pawn shops in a several-mile radius from his apartment.

He felt his phone buzz twice, notifying him of a new email. He stopped walking and moved away from the middle of the sidewalk to lean against a brick building. He pulled up the email on his phone and read it.

Lucas-

I can't tell you the pleasure I had reading your account of this demon. Of course, I would love to come and help you dispel this creature. Just one question - Would it be alright if I brought my camera crew? I am currently filming a season of a new series called 'The

Waiting Spirits,' and this would be the perfect season finale. Let me know ASAP, and I'll book a flight out.

Yours in spirit,

Isaiah Aquino

A camera crew? This guy couldn't be serious. Lucas knew a camera crew was the last thing that Kira would agree to - and Lucas understood completely. They'd have to perform caretaker duties, and allowing that to be shown on television was a certifiable terrible idea. The exposure, the questions, the media attention, the death threats by those who didn't believe in the afterlife, the death threats by those who thought they were insane - it was hardly an appealing way to live. Lucas closed the email and resumed his walk, contemplating the best way to try and avoid having a self-proclaimed exorcist and spirit banisher bring his damn camera crew.

An hour later, Lucas was not any closer to an idea for dealing with Isaiah Aquino, but as he walked down a block, he felt the chill of a spirit touch his skin. He paused. He was in front of one of the pawn shops along his route. This had to be the place. Lucas stowed his phone in his pocket and pulled out his strings. For good measure, he called on Rocko.

"What's happening, boss?" Rocko asked when he appeared at Lucas' side.

"Need to bind the spirit here," Lucas said.

"Sure thing."

Lucas pulled open the door to the pawn shop while Rocko simply passed through the brick wall. Inside, it was dark and dusty. An ancient-looking Indian man sat behind the counter, reading a worn book. The man looked up when Lucas entered and pushed his glasses up his nose.

"Buying or selling?" the man grunted.

"Browsing," Lucas answered. The man grunted again and turned his attention back to his book. As Lucas passed, he could see that the book was not written in English.

The shop was stuffed with various items that would probably never sell. Old electronics were stacked on shelves, teetering dangerously over the aisleways. Books overflowed boxes, and glass cases lined the walls filled with questionable jewelry, watches, and handguns. A semi-automatic rifle lay in one case. Lucas passed it by, wishing there were semi-automatic rifles capable of killing demons.

As Lucas wandered, he tried to feel for the presence of the spirit in the building. The chill clung to his skin, which was the only clue that he was in the right place. He stepped around a table strewn with once-popular children's toys and saw Rocko's shimmering form near a set of stairs at the back of the store.

"I think it's up there, boss," Rocko said. Lucas craned his head to get a look up the stairs. It was dark and dusty, just like the rest of the shop, and there was a closed door at the top, probably locked.

"Can you cause a distraction?" Lucas asked. Without giving an answer, Rocko moved across the store and managed to knock over a pile of electronics. The man behind the counter shot Lucas a nasty look, but Lucas just shrugged. The man closed his book with a snap, eased himself from the stool he sat on, edged around the counter, and stooped to pick up the electronics and pile them haphazardly back on the table. When the man's back was turned, Lucas rushed towards the steps and climbed them, trying to make as little noise as possible.

The wooden steps creaked during Lucas' entire ascension, but he made it to the top without incident. Before trying the door handle, Lucas glanced back down the steps to make sure the man hadn't noticed anything. At that moment, another crash sounded from below, and the man shouted in a different language. Rocko returned to Lucas.

"That should keep him busy," Rocko said and passed through the door. Lucas gripped the handle of the door and turned. To his surprise, it was unlocked, and he pushed open the heavy door and stepped through.

Chapter Fourteen

UNDINE

He emerged into a dusty attic. It was full of old furniture, old trunks and wardrobes, boxes of books, toys, rotting clothes, and in one corner, a piano. How anyone had gotten the piano into the attic was beyond him. But he ignored it. The important thing was that Lucas could now feel the spirit. He followed the feeling to the side of the attic opposite the piano.

"You're gonna need to cross over," Rocko said. "She's weak." Without hesitating, he closed his eyes and stepped through the barrier to the spirit realm.

When Lucas opened his eyes, he saw a young woman lying on the ground, her arms wrapped tightly around her legs. Her form was insubstantial, but he could make out her long pale hair, and her flowing gown of blue. She lifted her head to him when he appeared in front of her.

"Who?" she asked, her voice airy and soft. She sounded like she was very far away. A weak spirit, indeed.

"My name is Lucas. I'm a spirit caretaker. I'm here to take you away from here until you can pass over," he said, crouching down on his heels. He held a hand out to her.

"Cannot pass," she said.

"Huh?"

"Cannot pass over," she repeated. Beside him, Rocko made a noise.

"Why not?"

"Because a soul is required to pass over, and she doesn't have one," Rocko said, his voice tight. The woman lowered her head back to her knees as if she were resigned to remain in the attic for all eternity.

"How can she be a spirit if she has no soul?" Lucas asked.

"Undine," the woman said, her voice muffled further by her posture. Lucas repeated the word, but nothing came to mind. She lifted her gaze to him once more, and he could see that her eyes were a deep blue. "Water."

"Water? Are you an elemental?" Lucas asked. The woman didn't answer, so Lucas looked up at Rocko, who shrugged.

"How should I know? I just can tell she doesn't have a soul," Rocko said. Lucas sighed and held up the wad of strings in his hand.

"Look, I'm not sure if I can help you, but I can try," he said, addressing the woman. She stared at him, uncomprehending. "I bind you to this string, and I can take you away from his building." She perked up slightly at this. "May I?" The woman nodded her head vigorously. Lucas pulled an unused string between his fingers until it was taut. He spoke the words, and as he spoke, the string glowed. The woman uncurled her body and moved closer to Lucas. She reached out a hand and touched the string. For a moment, the spirit realm was blindingly bright, and the woman was gone. Lucas looked at the string between his fingers. He snorted in surprise. Rather than glowing white like the other spirits, this string glowed blue.

"That man is coming up the steps, boss," Rocko warned. Lucas tore his eyes from the blue string and shoved the wad in his pocket. He stepped back into the living realm.

The door at the top of the steps flew open, and the old man clamored through. "No one allowed up here!" he shouted at Lucas, who put up his hands, showing they were empty.

"Sorry. The door was unlocked, so I -"

"No one allowed up here. Leave now!" the man shouted. Lucas circled around the man, trying to keep a safe distance, and reached the steps. He hurried down, each of his heavy steps sending up a cloud of dust from the wood. Back on the ground floor, he didn't stop moving until he was out the door and back onto the street, striding quickly down the sidewalk. When he was several blocks away, he slowed his pace.

Lucas released a long breath and glanced around. He wasn't far from his favorite coffee shop, so he set off in that direction. While walking, he repeated the words 'undine' and 'water' in his mind, while Rocko's assertion that she had no soul echoed in his mind. Lucas pulled the strings from his pocket and glanced at them. Nestled among the white strings was the blue one, still glowing faintly. With his fingers hovering over the string, he was tempted to call her back out, but thought better of it. He wasn't sure he was ready to try and figure out this spirit or elemental or whatever she was, without attempting some research first.

At the coffee shop, he ordered a large black coffee and took up his usual spot in the corner armchair. He dropped his bag to the ground and pulled out his phone, which he used to access the internet. He began by searching the word 'undine.' The internet was quick to shed some light. The first result stated that undina or undine was the Latin term for an elemental water spirit. Lucas fished his strings from his pocket and separated the blue string from the rest. He couldn't feel much power coming from her and maybe, he was crazy, but perhaps she'd been away from water for too long. He stuffed his strings away when a woman walked by, eyeing him suspiciously.

He glanced back at his phone. He wasn't an expert on spirits, but he thought elementals were only from literature and myths. He hadn't been a believer in the afterlife before becoming a caretaker, so he supposed anything was possible at this point. He really should stop questioning anything strange.

A new email popped up on his phone. It was from Isaiah Aquino. Lucas read it over.

My producers are ecstatic about the idea of a demon episode. Please contact me ASAP.

-IA

Lucas rolled his eyes, but he mentally weighed the pros and cons. Maybe if they let this guy bring his camera crew, and they actually get rid of the demon, then they'd be rid of it without any cost to themselves, whether financial, mental, or spiritual. But if they did accept the idea of the guy bringing his crew, then Lucas and Kira would have to pretend that they're just amateur ghost hunters slash enthusiasts. He doubted that Kira would like that idea, but it was worth a try.

He sent her a text, asking her to come to the coffee shop when she had a chance, and added the address at the bottom.

Chapter Fifteen

PSEUDONYM

Three coffees and a bagel later, Kira walked through the doors of the shop. Her hair was pulled into a messy ponytail, and she was wearing worn jeans and a baggy hooded sweatshirt. Lucas raised an eyebrow. Usually, she was dressed up when she was out and about. He wondered if she was sick.

Kira spotted him and crossed the coffee shop, drawing glances from the other patrons. She plopped down in the armchair across from him and huffed, leaning back in the chair.

"Did you run here?" Lucas asked. Kira waved him off.

"Two poltergeists. Twins. I'm beat," she said.

"You could have called me," Lucas said. She lifted her head up and gave him a skeptical look.

"We're friends, not partners," she said rather blandly. Lucas' chest tightened unpleasantly, and he frowned.

"Wow, cold."

"That's not what I mean," she said, pushing herself up into a seated position. "What I do is dangerous, and you don't have the guarantee of coming back again if something happens. You're better off staying alive." Lucas stared at her, supposing he should be flattered that she cared about his safety, but he also wondered if she was just making things up. Lucas rose.

"I'm getting a refill. Do you want anything?" he asked.

"Just a black coffee," she said, her voice now sounding apologetic. Lucas gave her a smile. At least she had acceptable coffee preferences. He walked away from their corner and headed for the counter. The dreadhead barista smiled when he approached.

"You've never had a friend here before," the guy said, laughing. Lucas set his cup down and shook his head.

"Naw, I prefer to scare people by being a loner as much as possible," Lucas said. The guy laughed again. "Can I get a refill and a black coffee for the lady?"

"Sure thing, dude." Lucas waited while the barista retrieved his order. He glanced back at Kira, who was now curled up in the chair as if she might fall asleep. The barista set the cups down, and Lucas handed over the money. He took the cups back and pushed one into Kira's hands.

"You look beat," he said. Kira shrugged.

"You know how it goes," she said vaguely. Lucas did know.

"So, I have to talk to you about that Aquino guy," Lucas said once he'd sat back down. "I don't think you're going to like it."

"I didn't like this idea from the beginning," Kira said. She unfolded herself and sipped at her coffee.

"I know, but this is different. He wants to bring a camera crew along and film everything for the season finale of his show," Lucas said. Kira's eyes went wide.

"You're fucking kidding me, right?" she asked. "That's a terrible idea."

"I know," Lucas said. "But!" She glared at him. "Hear me out. We can just pretend to be amateurs who stumbled on something we clearly cannot handle. We don't have to tell him about caretakers."

"And what if he's a fraud?"

"Then we're really not any worse off than we were before, are we?" Lucas said. Kira set her cup aside and began to nervously twist the string from her hooded sweatshirt. At the very least, Lucas could tell she was contemplating the idea. "It's not like we care if he gets a good show from it or not," he added as a gentle nudge. Kira closed her eyes and released a long, slow sigh.

When she opened her eyes again, she said, "Alright, fine."

Isaiah Aquino worked quickly. And before the end of the day, he had arranged for himself and his crew to arrive in one week. Kira and Lucas were to meet him at the hotel he was staying at for initial interviews and discussions about what they found. Aquino also indicated that they'd have to sign a release statement about being on camera. As expected, Kira was furious.

"I don't want to be on camera!" she cried from Lucas' couch. "I'm not even supposed to be alive!" Lucas, leaning against his island counter with his arms crossed, raised his eyebrows.

"This is new," he commented. Kira froze.

"Uh…"

"Is Kira Sterling your real name?" he asked. Kira looked away.

"You'd be surprised how easy it is to let everyone believe you're dead, change your identity, and move to another city," she said, once again nervously twisting her sweatshirt strings. Lucas stared at her, waiting. "It was easier on my family," she said. "I couldn't let them keep believing that I was going to die only to come back to life. Plus, with my work… I just couldn't." For once, her expression changed from defiant to sad. Lucas uncrossed his arms and sat down beside her on the couch.

"I understand," he said. "You could have told me."

"You know that's not how I operate," she replied, still looking away from him.

"Well, you could always ask to be blurred out or something. Or maybe they can film you in shadow," Lucas said. "Or just let me do all the work." Finally, he saw a smile creep onto her lips.

"And let you have all the fun? Not a chance. I'll figure something out," she said.

Chapter Sixteen

WIG

The week passed quickly. Lucas joined Kira on a few of her spirit trappings and even convinced the child, Clark Kent, to pass over. Surprisingly, Margaret had been a big help, telling the boy about the afterlife as if she knew what lay beyond the space between life and death. But she lied well enough that Clark Kent was convinced that everything he ever wanted was on the other side, and he willingly passed. Lucas felt guilty about lying, but the weight released from having a child among his spirits was enough to counter the guilt.

On the morning of their interview with Isaiah Aquino, Kira showed up at Lucas' apartment early. From her bag, she pulled two sleek-looking boxes and set them on the counter.

"What are those?" Lucas asked.

"Wigs." She pulled open each box and lifted out a short red-orange bob and shoulder-length black hair. They were surprisingly realistic. She lifted both up beside her face. "Which is better?" Lucas laughed. "What?"

"Nothing. The lengths you go through…" he trailed off, noticing the shy smile on her face. "I think you'd look good with black hair since you're so pale. It'll look mysterious. And definitely the part of a weirdo ghost hunter." Kira stuck her tongue out at him and replaced the red-orange bob. She took the black wig to the bathroom, along with her bag.

Lucas finished his coffee. He walked to his bookshelf and pulled Aqunio's book from the shelf, and stuffed it in his messenger bag. He felt his spirits appear.

"What is it?" he asked, turning around. Margaret, Rocko, and Thomas were standing in a row.

"You're meeting that guy today?" Rocko asked.

"Yeah."

"Do you think that you'll go after the demon today, too?" Rocko asked. Lucas shrugged his shoulders.

"I have no idea what this guy's plan is," Lucas said. "Why?"

"We want to be there to help when you meet that demon again," Thomas said.

"It's too powerful."

"But it can't cross to the spirit world. We'll be there to make sure if anything happens, you cross over before it can hurt you," Margaret said, her voice oddly caring. "Rocko told us."

"I'm all for that," Lucas said. "But if this guy is legit, it's possible he might be able to sense you, or maybe he has instruments that can actually pick up on spirit energy. You have to be careful. We don't want him - one - thinking there are more ghosts to hunt and - two - getting mixed up between you and the demon. I'm sure we'll know more after we meet him. This is a total long shot."

"We'll be careful. Reis is going to be there too, keeping an eye on Kira," Rocko said.

"Good to know," Lucas said. Thomas and Rocko nodded and faded away while Margaret lingered for a moment.

"Don't forget about that water elemental. You need to deal

with her," Margaret said. Lucas couldn't tell if she was being rude or concerned. Before he could ask, she disappeared. He sighed and turned back to his bag.

A few minutes later, Kira emerged from the bathroom, looking transformed as a black-haired beauty. "How do I look?" she asked.

"Really good, actually," he said. The black hair brought out the whiteness of her skin in a lovely way. He tried hard not to stare. "Good enough to fool anyone who might be watching, I think." Kira patted the wig.

"Good." Lucas watched her for a moment as she walked back to the counter and set down her bag. She removed a few items, leaving them lined up neatly on the counter. The last thing she pulled out was a metal flask. She unscrewed the top and took a quick swing. Lucas cleared his throat.

"Really?" he asked. Kira glanced at him.

"I don't think you understand how far this is out of my comfort zone," she said. Lucas crossed his arms. "I didn't drink before driving over here." Lucas wasn't sure he believed her.

"I'm driving to the hotel."

"Fine." She took her keys from the bag and tossed them over. Lucas caught them and stuffed them in his pocket. She replaced her flask and threw the strap of her bag over her shoulder. "Stop judging me," she said with a scowl. "Friends aren't supposed to judge each other."

"Friends can judge each other a little bit," Lucas countered. Kira rolled her eyes. "Let's get moving." Lucas picked up his bag and led the way from his apartment. Down below, Kira had parked her car in the alley. They climbed inside, and Lucas started up the engine. In the passenger seat, Kira dug through her bag. Lucas pulled the car out of the alley and headed in the direction of the hotel. Kira pulled a spool of wire and a pair of wire cutters from her bag.

"Is that seriously how you make the threads for the spirits?" Lucas asked, glancing at her. She continued to measure out equal lengths of wire with her fingers, then snip the wire with her cutters.

"Part of it," she said. "Not all metals work for all spirits. I'm not even sure about this one. I couldn't find anything guaranteeing one hundred percent titanium."

"But you just cut pieces off a spool?" Lucas asked.

"The second part of the process is difficult," Kira said, still snipping. "I try to make a bunch at once so I don't have to do it all the time."

"What's the process?" Kira seemed to hesitate before she explained. Lucas waited.

"I have to cross to the spirit realm and, using a process that Dukaru taught me, split the wires into a physical wire and a spiritual wire," Kira began.

"What?"

"The spiritual wire remains on the spirit side, and I take the physical with me."

"This sounds impossible, even by caretaker physics," Lucas said.

"When a spirit is trapped in the wire," Kira went on, as if she didn't hear him speaking, "they are doubly trapped in the physical and spiritual world. They can't move until something is done with them. Then I either deliver the wires to Dukaru, or I leave the physical wires behind in the spirit world, trapping them there."

Kira stopped talking, still snipping wires. She now had a sizable pile in her lap. Lucas stared out the windshield, following his mental directions to the hotel. What she had just explained made no sense. He knew that being a caretaker meant relearning much of what one thought about the spirit world, but how could a piece of wire have a physical being and a spiritual being?

Lucas was about to ask Kira then when he glanced at her from the corner of his eye and closed his mouth. She had dropped the spool of wire and the cutters into her lap and was staring out the window of the car at the passing buildings and houses. He didn't think he was supposed to see, but there was a tear slowly rolling down her cheek. She ducked her head and wiped it away with the palm of her hand. This display only made him even more curious, and now, he felt worried that there was more that Kira wasn't telling him about her role as a spirit caretaker. A nagging thought formed in his head, and he began to think that this job of hers might literally be pulling her soul apart.

Chapter Seventeen

INTERVIEW

The hotel was not overly busy when they arrived. Lucas pulled into the semi-circle driveway at the front door and climbed out, leaving the car running. A few young men in slacks and polos were standing by the hotel valet podium, waiting for customers. A young man jogged up to them.

"How long will your stay be?" he asked. Lucas pulled a few dollars from his wallet and handed them over to the valet.

"Probably just a few hours," he said. The young man nodded and climbed into the driver's seat. Lucas joined Kira on the curb, and together, they walked through the double sliding doors into the hotel.

Aquino had sent an email to Lucas that morning that contained the room number where he and his crew would be operating. Now at the hotel, Lucas noted that the room number indicated that it was on the top floor. Probably a suite. Lucas wondered how much money this guy was making - this particular hotel wasn't one most regular people could afford.

Kira led the way across the hotel to the elevator, and together they stepped inside, and Lucas punched the button for the top floor.

"I'm nervous," Kira said. Lucas glanced at her, then put his hand gently on her shoulder and pulled her into a side hug.

"It'll be fine. If you want, I can do most of the talking," he said. Kira shrugged, but she seemed to relax slightly.

A soft bing preceded the doors sliding open on the top floor of the hotel. They stepped into the hallway together. There were only two doors off the landing - one to the right and one to the left. Lucas nodded towards the room on the right. They walked to the closed door and knocked.

From inside, they could hear many voices talking all at once, along with laughter. Finally, the door opened, revealing a short, thin man wearing all black. He had a clipboard tucked under his arm and a headset hanging around his neck.

"You must be Lucas and Kira," he said, smiling. He held out a hand to shake. "My name is Brett Underwood, director, and producer of The Waiting Spirits. We are so pleased to meet you and to have a chance to talk to you about your experience," Brett said, stepping inside to allow them into the suite. It was indeed a large room, with a few bedrooms that led off from the main room. There were already several cameras set up, along with bright stage lights and reflectors, all arranged around a grouping of three chairs and a coffee table. Most of the other furniture in the room had been pushed to the sides of the room to make way for other filming equipment. In one corner, several tables had been set up with food and coffee.

"May I?" Kira asked, gesturing towards the table.

"Oh, of course! Please, help yourselves!" Brett answered. Kira broke away and began to fill up two cups of coffee. Brett pulled his clipboard from under his arm and shuffled around a few pages. "I believe Isaiah informed you that you'd have to sign a release in order to appear on film?"

"He did."

"Excellent, and you're both okay with that?"

"Yeah."

Brett smiled and pulled two pieces of paper from his clipboard and produced two pens from a pocket. He handed these to Lucas. "Go ahead and read through these, and sign at the bottom. If you have any questions, please let me know."

Brett stepped away, walking towards an arrangement of computers and small television monitors. Kira returned to Lucas' side and pressed a cup of coffee into his hands.

"Thanks. Ready to sign?" he asked. Kira sighed and took the form from Lucas. They both scanned the document, which contained all the information that Lucas had expected to see. Using a nearby table, they both signed their forms.

There was still quite a bit of activity in the room. Several people, all wearing black, were still arranging the equipment or making minute adjustments to the equipment that was already set up. Most of them ignored Lucas and Kira.

"I wonder where Aquaman is," Kira whispered. Lucas chuckled and shook his head.

"I'm just wondering how much of a diva he is," Lucas said. "I got the sense from his emails that he has an inflated ego."

"Why? It's not like this is mainstream shit," Kira commented. "Most people with a brain don't believe in any of this crap."

"That's ironic, coming from you," Lucas said, and Kira gave him a questioning look. "Considering you know a lot of it is real." Kira shrugged and looked away.

"I don't think these people could handle reality."

"Maybe not," Lucas said to appease her.

One of the doors opened, and the man, that must be Isaiah Aquino, stepped out. Lucas nudged Kira. He was very tall and much broader than his pictures on the Internet seemed to indicate. Lucas thought he had the physical structure of a professional football player. Aquino was wearing a black button-down shirt and a white tie over black pants. Several silver-colored rings adorned Aquino's fingers.

After Aquino stepped from the room, his eyes immediately landed on the two people whose faces he didn't immediately recognize. He smiled, revealing brilliantly white teeth. He spread his arms wide and crossed the large room towards Lucas and Kira, easily passing through the activity that continued around him.

"You must be my new friends!" he said as he neared them. Lucas heard Kira suppress a snort. "I am Isaiah Aquino." He stopped in front of them and held out his hand. Lucas was the first to shake his hand, which was dwarfed by Aqunio's massive size. Kira shook his hand next, and her slim hand disappeared inside Aqunio's grip.

"Lucas Harrison."

"Kira Sterling."

Aquino smiled and spread his arms once again. "I can't even begin to tell you how pleased I am that you contacted me, Lucas. I had just been discussing with Brett what kind of episode we could put together for the season finale when your email appeared, and I said, 'This is perfect!' Brett is excited as well. We think that this will really help us wrap up the show and leave the viewers wanting more," Aquino said. Lucas was about to thank Aquino for his praises when Kira spoke up first.

"Do you really know what you're doing here?" she asked, a little harsher than necessary. Aquino's gaze never lost its glittering amusement.

"I have been learning the ways of banishing spirits for a long time," Aquino said, still with a smile. "Even if this demon proves to be a challenge, we can leave this episode off as a cliffhanger."

Lucas winced inwardly at his comment, and he could feel Kira's rage building. Luckily for Aquino, Brett called him over for a mic check. Lucas turned and stood in front of Kira after Aquino stepped away. He put his hands on her shoulders.

"Calm down," he said. Kira glared at him.

"This guy is a fraud. There's no way he really knows what he's doing," Kira said, her voice a low, aggressive whisper. "He only cares about getting good material for his stupid show."

"I know," Lucas said. He stepped closer to Kira, closing the distance between them. "But we agreed we'd go through with this, just to see if he really knows what he's doing. We are just playing the parts of two amateur ghost hunters who found something really weird."

"I know, but-"

"At the very least, Rocko and Reis will be able to protect us if anything goes wrong." At this, Kira sighed and deflated a bit.

"Alright," she conceded. Lucas pulled her into a quick hug. When he released her, Brett appeared.

"If you two are ready, we can go ahead and mic you up," he said. They both nodded and stepped into the swarm of activity. The little black lapel mics were attached to their shirts, and the battery packs were attached to their pants' waistbands. The audio guy asked them to talk at normal levels into the mics while he adjusted the sound. Finally, Kira and Lucas were asked to sit down in the two chairs, which were angled towards a third chair. Aquino noticed them sitting and excused himself from the conversation he was having. He dropped down into the third chair.

"This will be the easy part," he said, leaning forward with his elbows resting on his knees. "We'll just talk about how you came across this demon and what you experienced. Be as detailed as possible, and don't worry if you mess up. A lot can be corrected in post-production." He smiled.

"Ready, Mr. Aquino?" Brett asked from his place beside one of the cameras. Aquino nodded. "Sterling and Harrison interview, take 1-"

Aquino introduced them as ghost enthusiasts, and Lucas found it easy to fall into conversation. Kira remained silent through most of the interview, only interjecting when she felt it was necessary. Lucas knew she was content to let him deal with explaining the story without giving away any of their secrets. It helped that Lucas read widely on the subject of ghosts and hauntings, and he and Aquino were able to fall into some easy banter.

Lucas thought he had given a stirring rendition of the encounter with the demon. The crew and Aquino all seemed to be leaning forward closer to him, listening intently. Even Kira was swept up in the story, and she had been there. Naturally, he left out the parts about the spirit world and Reis and Rocko. When he finished his story, Aquino gave his interpretation of the event, including his assurance that this was a genuine encounter with an otherworldly being. Lucas glanced at Kira and saw that she was smirking, apparently to keep herself from laughing.

Chapter Eighteen

H(A)UNTING

Despite Aquino's excitement, the filming of the demon had to wait until the following day. They hadn't yet gotten permission from the city to film in the abandoned building, and the city didn't seem quite convinced by Aquino's reasons.

Lucas was lounging in his bed when he got a call from the director, Brett Underwood.

"Lucas! Good morning! We're clear to shoot the next part of the episode. Can you and Kira meet us down at the location? We can send a car if needed."

"Sure, send a car," Lucas said and gave Underwood the address. Lucas hung up the phone and sent a text to Kira, letting her know of the plan. She took her time responding back but said she would meet at his apartment.

Lucas dressed in his most ghost-hunter-ish outfit - a black hooded sweatshirt featuring the art and name of a metal band and black cargo pants - remnants from his less fashion-conscious days. He shook out his shaggy hair and sent a comb through his beard. Good enough.

Soon, the bell to his apartment rang, and Lucas pressed the button to unlock the door below. Kira clomped up the steps. She apparently had the same idea as he: she wore a dark pair of jeans, a black hooded sweatshirt, and what appeared to be heavy combat boots. She wore her black wig already and had done up her makeup. Lucas smiled.

"You almost look like a regular goth chick," Lucas commented. Kira scrunched her nose at him but smiled anyway.

"It's a good disguise, yeah?" she asked, spinning in an unsteady circle.

"I think it'll work," Lucas said. Kira patted her wig and smiled. Lucas wandered to the window and looked down. A sleek, black sedan was parked in front of the sex toy shop. Lucas watched as the driver climbed out of the car and checked his phone, then looked up at the third floor of the building.

"I think our ride is here," Lucas said. He turned away from the window and headed towards the door, Kira following. They descended the steps to the street. The driver saw them appear from around the corner and hailed them.

"You Lucas Harrison?" the driver asked. Lucas waved to him and nodded. "Great. Let's go."

The driver slipped back into the car while Kira and Lucas climbed into the back seat. The interior of the car was all leather and was already deeply cool from the air conditioning. Lucas settled back in the seat while Kira perched on the edge. The driver pulled away from the curb and headed in the direction of the abandoned building.

Lucas glanced at Kira. "Don't be nervous," he said. Kira glanced at him warily.

"This is dangerous," she replied. "We don't know what will happen. Someone could get seriously hurt. Especially," her voice dropped low. "If he's a fraud."

Lucas sighed. He couldn't deny that she was right, but he got the feeling from Aquino that perhaps he had more up his sleeve than being some sensationalist ghost hunter. The longer Lucas held the role as a caretaker of spirits, the less skeptical he was of people who were sensitive to the afterlife. He'd certainly seen stranger things than a normal human who could actually commune with the dead.

The rest of the ride passed in silence. Kira had relaxed enough to lean back against the seat and look out the window while Lucas played a game on his phone to pass the time. Eventually, the car pulled down the street where the abandoned building stood and pulled along the curb behind several other vans. The crew was already busy unloading film equipment onto the sidewalk and into the foyer of the building.

Lucas spotted Aquino dressed in an outfit that appeared vaguely like something a Catholic priest would wear. Like a badly put-together costume. Lucas grimaced, and he heard Kira mumble something under her breath.

"Ah! There you are!" Aquino said, spotting the two of them. He walked over, his arms spread wide as if he intended to envelop the two of them into a hug. Thankfully, he dropped his arms to his sides when he reached them, and instead settled on shaking their hands. Brett Underwood appeared at Aquino's side, a clipboard in his hand.

"We need to know which floor you were on when you saw this creature," Brett said. "We want to send the crew up to get some b-roll."

"The twentieth floor," Lucas said.

"And the elevators don't work," Kira added with mirth in her voice. Brett's face fell for a moment, but he shrugged and turned to the waiting crew.

"Floor twenty! Get moving!"

The crew groaned but went on their way. Aquino watched all this with a smile.

"I can't tell you how excited I am," he said. "This is going to be a great ending, and I know the network will renew us for a second season. And maybe…" he said, tapping his finger against his chin. "Maybe we can have you as recurring characters."

Lucas and Kira exchanged a glance.

"I don't know about that," Lucas said, but Aquino waved him off.

"We can discuss semantics later. For now, let's get to hunting this demon!"

He whirled around and strode down the sidewalk towards the front door of the building. Lucas and Kira followed after him at a much less chipper pace.

Chapter Nineteen

JOHN 8:44

After the trek to the twentieth floor of the office building, Lucas and Kira were out of breath. So were Aquino, Underwood, and the rest of the crew who had to carry the heavy filming equipment. The crew took a ten-minute break, leaning against the dusty walls, to recover from the climb before continuing with the shoot. In the meantime, Lucas and Kira walked down the hall to the room where they'd first encountered the demon.

Lucas felt Rocko and Thomas appear beside him, and he also felt the presence of several spirits that belonged to Kira. Their energies were nervous and on edge.

"It's here," Rocko whispered to Lucas. Kira shifted on her feet. Lucas could feel the energy of the demon pulsating, but he couldn't quite figure out where it was coming from. The room the demon had been in before was empty of energy.

"He must be further down the hall," Kira said. Lucas nodded and followed her down to the next door. The crew behind them perked up and scrambled to get their cameras and microphones working.

Aquino pushed through the crew and jogged to catch up with the two of them. He turned and waited for a moment, walking backward, until Underwood gave him a thumbs up.

"Here we are on the twentieth floor of this abandoned building, where we're tracking the scent of the demon. So far, we haven't seen any signs, but I'm confident that we'll encounter this demonic energy before the night is out," Aquino said to the cameras. He turned back around and hurried to Kira and Lucas. He grasped their shoulders and whispered, "I feel him. Do you?"

Lucas and Kira both nodded. Lucas had a hunch that Aquino was only feeling the gathered spirits that hung around Kira and himself.

"Such an evil energy," Aquino whispered. Lucas shuddered. The evil energy was closer now and angrier.

Lucas was about to ask Kira if she felt anything when the ground beneath them began to shake. Several cries erupted from the gathered crew as they were flung from their feet onto the ground. Lucas grabbed at the wall, trying to steady himself, while his other hand flew out and grasped Kira by the bicep. She wrapped her own hand around his wrist.

The shaking stopped. Lucas and Kira stared at each other. They both knew what this meant - the demon was extremely strong and extremely angry.

Lucas turned to Aquino and was going to tell him they needed to leave when a voice materialized from the air, speaking in a gravelly voice. Lucas thought the voice was speaking in Latin again.

"It's here!" Aquino shouted, turning to his crew. "I hope you're getting this!"

The crew scrambled to their feet, fumbling with their equipment. Lucas and Kira pressed their backs against the wall, and Kira rummaged through her bag until she withdrew her hand. Clutched between her fingers were several pieces of her titanium wire. He wondered what the chances were that those pieces of wire would actually trap a demon.

The voice stopped speaking, and the air became deathly quiet.

No one moved. Lucas felt the quivering of his spirits around him, vibrating with fear and anticipation.

A blast of hot air pushed down the hall, forcing Lucas onto his back. Kira and Aquino landed on top of Lucas. The gust whipped through the hallway, pulling equipment from the hands of the crew and tossing it aside. A maniacal laughter cut through the silence. Lucas struggled to move out from under Aquino and Kira, who were struggling themselves. Finally, he freed himself and climbed to his feet. He reached down and pulled Kira to her feet. They turned towards the end of the hallway and gasped.

The demon was there. It stood at the end of the hall, its form hunched over, breathing heavily. Red ooze dripped from its teeth that stuck out of its horse-like mouth. It opened its mouth and began to speak in Latin once more.

"What's it saying?" Lucas asked, shaking with fear. Kira shook her head.

"He's reciting John 8:44," Aquino said. He'd pulled himself from the floor and was standing behind Lucas and Kira. "You belong to your father, the devil, and you want to carry out your father's desires. He was a murderer from the beginning, not holding to the truth, for there is no truth in him. When he lies, he speaks his native language, for he is a liar and the father of lies."

Lucas and Kira exchanged glances. Aquino pushed past the two and stepped forward, his arms outstretched. In Lucas' mind, he saw Jesus nailed to the cross.

"Submit, demon!' Aquino said. "You have no place in the world of the living. Return from whence you came! You have no power here!"

The demon laughed again, and another gust of hot, stinking air blew down the hall. This time, Lucas, Kira, and Aquino braced themselves and remained on their feet.

"No power, indeed," the demon said, speaking English for the first time. The demon lurched forward. It sped down the hallway and collided with Aquino, who screamed out and fell backward. Lucas and Kira ducked out of the way. Aquino landed on his back on the ground, his eyes closed.

"Shit," Kira mumbled. They turned and saw that the demon swept down the entire hall, knocking Aquino's crew to the ground once more. Their equipment was busted into pieces. The demon stood on the other end of the hall, grinning a terrible grin. Lucas clenched his hands into fists.

"We've got to do something," Lucas said.

"I know." Kira held out her titanium wires and waved her hand toward the demon. "Get him!" Her spirits, along with Lucas' spirits, flew down the hall and crashed into the demon. Powerful surges of energy blasted down the hall and in all directions. The building shook to its very foundation.

Kira stepped forward, holding the metal wires between her hands. Lucas called after her to stop, but she ignored him. Over the sounds of the clashing spirits and demons, he could hear her chanting something in Latin.

The demon screeched and lashed out its arms, trying to fling away the spirits. Lucas could feel the spirits disappearing from the living realm, one by one. Kira kept walking towards the demon, muttering her Latin incantation. The wires in her hands glowed a deep red color.

"Back away, girl! You have no power over me!" the demon shouted. Kira ignored the demon's words, chanting and holding the wires in front of her. Kira stopped moving and shouted the last bit.

"Get in the damn wire!"

The demon cried out, half laughing, half screaming, but Lucas could see that its form was fading, and the oppressive evil was dissipating. The wires glowed brighter and brighter until Kira took a deep breath and stepped forward. Her form disappeared. She'd gone into the spirit realm. Lucas took a hasty step forward and passed through the barrier as well.

On the other side, he saw Kira wrestling with the wires, tying several of them into knots. A ghostly image of the demon hovered above her, fighting against her power.

"Stop. Moving." Kira drew another wire from her bag and added it to the knotted wires in her hand. The demon screamed so loud Lucas had to cover his ears to keep his eardrums from erupting. And just as quickly, the scream stopped. Kira pushed the wires from her hand, and they landed in a knotted heap on the ground. The metal wires melted and fused together. Kira grasped at her hand. Lucas ran to her side and looked. Her hand sported a large welt that was bubbled and burst. It was a bad burn and would need medical treatment.

"Come on. Leave it here," Lucas said, pulling on her shoulder. Kira shook her head.

"Not done yet," she said. She looked around the spirit realm and shouted, "Dukaru!"

They waited, but the grim reaper didn't show up. No one showed up. Kira scoffed and kicked at the bundle of melted wires. It sizzled against the floor, glowing red.

"Just leave it here," Lucas said. Kira stared hard at it but finally nodded. Together, they stepped through the barrier and back into the living realm.

Chapter Twenty

BURN

Back in the living realm, Kira fell to her knees, her burned hands clutched to her chest. Lucas could see on her face that she was in pain. He knelt beside her and placed a hand on her shoulder. He could feel her body shaking.

"Are you alright?" he asked. Kira shook her head and allowed herself to lean into his shoulder for support. Lucas wrapped an arm around her. "Do you need to go to the hospital?" he asked.

"Maybe for my hands, but I can't get up yet," she muttered.

Around them, the rest of Aquino's crew began to stir. They opened their eyes and blinked, raising themselves up from the ground. They spoke to each other in low whispers, wondering what the hell had happened.

Aquino himself roused and stood. He looked around, frowned at his scattered crew, and his eyes fell on Lucas and ira.

"What happened?" he asked. "The demonic energy is gone."

"Not gone," Kira said. "Trapped."

Aquino took a step towards them, eyeing them suspiciously.

"What do you mean... trapped? What did you do?"

Kira winced against Lucas' hold, realizing that she'd said too much. Neither of them answered Aquino's question.

"You're not just ghost hunters, are you?" he asked, moving closer to them, keeping his voice low. "What are you?"

"We can't say," Lucas finally said, glancing up at Aquino to meet his gaze. Aquino gave Lucas a quizzical look, his mouth set in a firm line. Finally, after an awkward silence, Aquino's expression softened, and he knelt down beside the two of them.

With his voice low, he said, "Your secret, whatever it is, is safe with me," he said. With that, he rose and turned to his crew. Brett Underwood jogged up to Aquino, having found his clipboard and papers scattered about the hallway.

"Looks like this episode will have to end on a cliffhanger," Aquino said.

"What do you mean?" Brett asked.

"The demon has disappeared."

"Isaiah..."

"Let's watch the film that we did get and wrap the episode up tomorrow. Maybe we got something good enough to cut into a reasonable ending," Aquino said.

Brett shifted on his feet, clutching his clipboard against his chest.

"Are you sure about this?" he asked. Aquino nodded.

"Now, let's get out of here. It looks like our crew could use a drink," he said. Brett stared at Aquino for a moment before turning around to the crew and waving his arm in a circle above his head.

"Alright, everyone, pack it up. Let's go!" he called.

Lucas helped pull Kira to her feet, though she leaned most of her weight against him. Lucas wasn't looking forward to the twenty flights of stairs.

* * *

Lucas, Kira, Aquino, and the crew made their way down, down, down the steps of the building, eventually landing in the lobby. The crew made for the vans to pack up their equipment. Aquino lingered behind, waiting for Lucas and Kira.

When they reached him, he held out a hand. Lucas shook it.

"I'd like to keep in touch," Aquino said. "If you ever come up against something you can't handle, give me a call."

"What, and be another episode of your show?" Kira asked through clenched teeth. Aquino shook his head.

"No. My show - it's all smoke and mirrors with a little bit of paranormal sensitivity. This is real," he said. "I am trained in exorcisms, but when the Catholic church found out about my unsanctioned rituals, they excommunicated me. I've developed my own ritual away from the church and have found it to be somewhat effective, depending on the strength of the demon."

Kira and Lucas exchanged a glance.

"He could be useful in the future," Lucas said, shrugging his shoulders. Kira stared at Aquino for a moment, then relented and held out a hand to shake his. Aquino's face lit up, and he vigorously returned the handshake.

"I'll send you both a check in the mail for your participation," Aquino said. "It's the least I can do for dragging you into this whole thing. I honestly thought this might be a hoax that I could at least use as a good story."

"Wouldn't blame you for that," Kira said. Aquino smiled at Kira and turned halfway toward his working crew.

"Like I said, keep in touch," he said and nodded to them. Kira and Lucas raised a hand in farewell. Aquino walked away.

Lucas glanced down at Kira. "Well, let's get you to the hospital," he said. Kira wrinkled her nose but nodded. Blisters were already forming on her hands, red and bulbous. Lucas winced at how painful they looked. Lucas led Kira from the building towards her parked car.

Chapter Twenty-One

MYSTERY

A roll of bandages and a tub of salve later, Kira and Lucas were driving through the city, Kira in the passenger seat, directing Lucas on where to turn. After a while, he recognized the area as being the location of the warehouse where Kira had first taken him to meet Dukaru. Sure enough, Kira directed him into a parking lot of a large, deserted warehouse. Lucas parked the car outside the main door. They climbed from the car.

"Dukaru isn't going to be happy about this," Kira said, pulling the chains from the door handles.

"What can he do about it?"

"I don't know. Probably nothing."

Kira pulled open the doors, which squeaked and creaked on their hinges. Together, they stepped into gloom. Their footsteps echoed through the cavernous space, kicking up dirt and other debris that had been left on the floor when the building was abandoned. Kira stopped walking and glanced to Lucas.

"Ready to cross over?" she asked. He nodded, and together they took a breath and stepped forward, brushing through the veil between the living and the spirit realm.

Kira didn't have to call for Dukaru. He was already waiting on the other side. And for a skeletal creature with no discernable features, he looked pissed.

"What did you do?" he asked, gravel dripping from his voice. Kira took a step forward.

"I had to do something," Kira argued.

"That demon was not bothering anyone," Dukaru said. "You should have left it alone."

"Someone wanted me to find that demon, otherwise, I wouldn't have gotten the message," Kira said. Dukaru didn't respond right away. The arms of his robe crossed over his chest.

"It wasn't anyone of mine," Dukaru said.

"Someone sent the message," Kira said. "And I trapped the demon. I don't know what to do with it, so now it's in your hands."

A sound emitted from Dukaru, chilling Lucas to the bone. After a moment, Lucas realized that Dukaru was laughing. Lucas couldn't help but clench his fists together in a tight ball.

"Stupid girl," Dukaru said, still laughing. "This will be your problem forever. The demon will be tied to you for the rest of your life." Kira and Lucas exchanged a glance and blinked. How was that even possible? All Kira did was trap the demon in the wire. "You don't have the power to exorcise demons. All you did was create a temporary cage. But the demon will free itself eventually, and when it does, it will come after you." Lucas jumped when he felt Kira slip her hand into his. She squeezed his palm with her fingers out of fear or perhaps anger. Dukaru stopped laughing, and the void of his face stared directly at Kira. "Good luck."

In a whirl of dust and leaves, Dukaru vanished. Lucas shook his head and returned a squeeze to Kira's hand. Kira bit her lip and turned away.

"Let's cross back over," she said, pulling her hand away from Lucas'. He immediately felt the absence of her hand, and he frowned.

Together, they took a deep breath and stepped across the divide into the living realm. Without waiting for him, Kira stormed through the warehouse towards the door, which she shoved open with her bandaged hands. Lucas hurried after her, his bag bumping against his leg as he ran.

Outside in the fading light, Lucas called after Kira to stop. She only stopped moving when she reached her car. Lucas approached her, his hands held out in front of him, palms spread.

"It'll be okay," he said. "Even if the demon does come back, we'll figure out a way to trap him again. Everything will be fine-"

Kira cut him off with a wave of her hand.

"You think I'm worried about some demon?" she asked, losing control of the volume of her voice. Lucas took a step back, lowering his hands to his sides.

"Then what-"

"Someone… or… something knows how to contact me. They know how to tell me where to find spirits. Someone is purposely sending me into dangerous situations. If it's not Dukaru, then who is it?"

Lucas opened his mouth to respond, but he had no words. Instead, he stepped forward and roughly grabbed Kira's bandaged hands in his own.

"We'll figure this out. Don't worry." Kira scowled at him.

"You don't know anything about what I've gone through," she said, trying to pull herself backward, but Lucas held firm. He could see in her eyes that tears had sprung. He softened his expression and touched her cheek with one hand.

"Whether you like it or not, we're friends now, Partners, even. I'll be here for you, and we'll figure out who is sending you these messages, and we'll deal with the demon if it ever comes back. I'm not going to let anything happen to you."

A tear fell to Kira's cheek, and Lucas wiped it away. She pulled her hand from his and threw her arms around his neck, pulling him into a rough hug. Lucas lowered his hands to her back and pulled her against his chest. He closed his eyes, and when he did, he saw fire.

END OF BOOK ONE

About the Author

N.C. MADIGAN

If you enjoyed this book, don't forget to leave a review!

N.C. Madigan is a speculative fiction author. She enjoys the three Bs-- Books, Bourbon, and Board Games. She lives in Michigan with her boyfriend, her dog, and her snake.

Connect with her:

Instagram: @ncmadigan
TikTok: @ncmadigan
Facebook: N.C. Madigan

www.ncmadigan.com

www.ingramcontent.com/pod-product-compliance
Lightning Source LLC
Chambersburg PA
CBHW060943120626
46557CB00003B/1115